ONCE UPON A
WARTIME III

by Molly Burkett

ISBN N° 0 948204 17 6

Text © Molly Burkett
All rights reserved. No part of this publication may be
reproduced or transmitted in any form or by any means
without prior permission of the publisher.

Published by **BARNY BOOKS**
Hough-on-the-Hill • Grantham • Lincs

Produced by **TUCANN***design&print*
19 High Street • Heighington • Lincoln LN4 1RG
Telephone & Fax: 01522 790009

Signed By.
Peter. E. Compton-Sandy.
Lt. Comdr, Ex RN

Once Upon A Wartime III

Vught, Holland during the War

They weren't too bad at first, the Germans that is. They tried to be friendly but we weren't having any of it. There were some that did. We had our quislings the NSB (National Socialist Party) lead by Mussert. They wore black uniforms and some of them were worse than the Nazis. We had nothing to do with them and kept out of their way.

We lived just outside Vught in Southern Holland. I was seventeen. I had left school and was working as a clerk in the law courts when the Germans came. The tanks came first and then the soldiers with horse and carts. They were crazy for the chocolates and soaps in the shops. To them they were luxuries. Hitler had been so keen to spend all the available money on his war machine and autobahns that there wasn't any left for luxuries. They would stand in the streets and eat packets of butter as if they were bars of chocolate.

My sister was two years older than me. I had another sister who was married with two children in the north of the country and a brother who was a solicitor. My other brother was in the Dutch navy. We had no idea what happened to him when the Germans overan Holland until my mother heard a message from him on the radio. It was her birthday. She never listened to the radio as a rule, but she did that day and she heard his message and that was how we knew he had joined up with the British navy. He had simply come home one day, packed some clothes and kissed his wife goodbye and said he might be away for a while. He didn't even tell her where he was going. Later we had messages from him through the Red Cross.

The first thing the Germans did was to confiscate all our radios, but we hid one under the floorboards. That was how we knew what was going on. They confiscated bicycles as well, so there was a rush to get wooden wheels fitted onto our bikes. The Germans didn't want those.

At first we could move about Holland without any trouble, but that soon changed. We had identity cards and had to carry them with us. Food, clothes, everything was rationed, even electricity. We were allowed one small electric light bulb for so many hours a day. There was a curfew and we made sure we were home and safe before it started. You could be taken off at a moment's notice. I was called up for labour camp like most of the men in my age group were. These labour camps were like prison camps where you had to do war work for the Germans. You could write home but you weren't allowed to go there and you had to wear a green uniform. I couldn't go though because I went down with scarlet fever and I never heard from them again. Lots of my friends had to go and it was five years before they saw their families again.

All Dutch officers had to report to the Germans and they were sent to prisoner of war camps. Then the soldiers followed them. The Jews were ordered to wear a yellow star. We didn't like that. We knew what had happened to the German Jews, so we all wore a yellow star until the Germans announced that everyone wearing a yellow star would be sent to concentration camps. Well none of us were that brave. Lots of the Jews went into hiding. There were some Jewish families that stayed hidden throughout the war. There were brave people who sheltered them or even helped them because they were shot if they were discovered. There was a Jewish family in the flat beneath my brother and they asked him to look after their valuables and they would return to get them after the war. Someone reported the Jewish family and the Sicherheits polizei (the secret police) found them, they also found a list of their valuables and where they had left them and turned up at my brother's flat and demanded them. They made them all get out of bed and made them stand with guns trained on them, even the children. My brother tried to deny knowledge of them at first, but they knew he had them. They found them and took them and my brother away. They let him go after twenty four hours but he was really shaken.

They built a concentration camp at the edge of the village. It was for political prisoners and members of the resistance. They wore old Dutch army uniforms with a red patch if they were political prisoner and a lilac one if they were priests. Then they had a striped uniform like all the other inmates of concentration camps.

We had four barracks at Vught. The SS was in the concentration camp. They were evil. They said that some of them were murderers that had been released from prison. They had a dreadful reputation.

The Panzers had a barracks in the town and there were two other barracks. When they first came they thought they really were masters of the world. They didn't expect anyone to stand in their way. They showed us their orders and it was written down where they were to report in England. They'd got it all planned out.

It was like a dark shadow having that concentration camp. They started taking the Jews there and allied aircrews. There were some Canadian airmen there too.

They were forced to work. They needed bricks for the blockhouses and we used to watch the lines of prisoners from the camp being forced to walk five miles to the docks and back again at night, in all weathers. Some of them didn't have shoes and none of them had proper clothing. At five o'clock every evening the shooting started. We could hear it from our house. They had a ditch with a bank and the prisoners were made to stand on this bank and then they were shot. Ten minutes later an officer would march over and shoot any that had not been killed with his revolver. The SS seemed to treat it like a game. The resistance made holes under the wire and they would wriggle in and fetch out some of the prisoners who hadn't been killed. They were brave men. Tommy Arts, was one of the resistance rescued after he had been shot. He went on to work with my sister, typing up the German records.

Tommy couldn't contact his family and let them know he was alive. If the Germans learned how he had been rescued, they would have stopped others being saved in the same way. They could have laid a trap and caught the resistance workers. Meanwhile his parents had been notified that he had been shot and they were mourning his death.

The Germans were methodical and systematic. They kept details of everything that happened at the camp. Somehow the resistance got the records out and my sister and others typed them out. Most of it was typing out the names of the Jewish prisoners. They could only work for thirty minutes at a time, because it made them sick, physically sick. The Germans did some terrible things to those prisoners. The women were as bad as the men if not worse. They used to skin the prisoners while they were still alive and use the skin to make lampshades. It's all written down there. I couldn't tell you some of the things that they did to the prisoners but they wrote down every detail.

They took prisoners to the station and loaded them into cattle trucks for Dachau. We knew what was going on but there was nothing we could do to stop it. We tried to distance ourselves from the Germans. Children were told never to talk to them. We went out of our way to avoid them, but you could never get away from their presence. They were always marching through the streets, marching and singing and there was always the concentration camp which we had to pass every day. I must be fair to the Germans though. They were well disciplined. If they raped a Dutch girl, they were shot. Mind you it wasn't the same for the poor Jewish girls in the camp. You can guess how they were treated and many of them became pregnant. When they grew near their time and they were of no further use, they were tossed into these vats of burning oil. The Germans wrote it all down in these reports, as if they were proud of it.

As the war progressed, they became short of labour and they rounded up the people in the streets and carted them off. You hardly dared walk down the street. All sorts and ages of people were being taken., I got some false papers claiming I was a mechanic. That would exempt me from forced labour. All the same I kept out of the way. Lots of young people went underground. Then I was stopped and my papers were studied for a long time before I was allowed to go. I didn't stop shaking for two days after that. We lived with fear.

"Yes," his sister interrupted, "I can tell you my most frightening experience. I was cycling home and I was rushing to get indoors before the curfew and this German caught up with me and cycled alongside me. He started being suggestive and objectionable and I had to get away from him, so I gave him a shove and called him a German pig, only I had started taking English lessons and I had blurted it out in English without thinking. Well I hardly dared go out of the house after that, but I was lucky. He had been too drunk to remember much."

We had to be alert every minute of the day because we lived under threat. I worked at the town hall. Young women of my age group had to work although it was unusual for girls from our background to go out to work. Our boss was an ex Dutch army officer although none of us were supposed to know that. Somebody had mentioned that he worked for the resistance but that was something we didn't want to know.

I worked with a really nice girl, but she was fond of men and she had a German boyfriend. One day she lost her temper and started to shout at the manager. She threatened him and told him that she was going to tell her boyfriend all about him. We were horror struck. We went and told one of the resistance workers what had happened and when we returned, the manager had disappeared. He had been whisked away for his own protection. He didn't come back to the office.

We had our fun. We would have dances in friends houses, but they would have to be all night affairs because of the curfew. We seemed to live a normal life on the surface, but underneath was the fear, fear of what the Germans could do and a feeling of horror and helplessness. As the war went on food became more and more difficult. At first we had been able to get food from farms but most of their produce had to go to the Germans and some of the farmers started to get greedy, wanting jewellery or clothes in exchange for eggs or apples.

Then it was September 17th 1944. One of the resistance was sitting at our table for a long time it seemed to us. Then he heard the sound of an engine. He stood up and said quietly, "I must go now". We followed him out and the sky was alive. At first the planes came in high and dropped the gliders and parachutists. Then they came in real low and the crews were standing in the doorways waving and we were waving and shouting back. Then there was one plane that circled the village several times, tipping its wing on one side and dipping over the big house and we knew it was Rob Bergman. He'd been one of a group of students who had got out and made their way to England. I don't know how Rob had become a pilot in the RAF, but we all knew it was him. One of the gliders came down in a village nearby. There was a jeep in it and some soldiers. The resistance helped get it out and pointed out where the rest of the allied soldiers were and they drove right through the village, right through the Germans and not one of them tried to stop them. The Germans were completely bemused. They did not know what was happening.

Operation Market Garden, Arnhem, some say it was a failure but not us. It gave us hope and told us that we were not forgotten by the rest of the world.

There was shooting getting nearer and the Germans were strengthening their defences in the village. We slept in a friend's house in the village because they had deep cellars. The cellar was packed. The Germans had an anti tank gun in the house next door. The foundations shook. We had no idea what was going on. Then in the middle of the battle, we heard this weird sound and it seemed to be getting louder. Well I was running up the steps to get out of the cellar. The others were following and down the road was coming the Black Watch, playing the bagpipes. They were walking down the street as if they were out for an afternoon stroll. Behind them came the Welsh Guards in single file on either side of the road. Well, we were laughing and shouting and the battle was still going on around us and we didn't care. The British Officer was pleading with us to take cover. He said we'd get killed. He kept asking us to take shelter, but we didn't care. We didn't care.

We were lucky. It took another five weeks before the village next to us was liberated. The fighting was so fierce.

Food started to get better after that, but it was many years before rationing ended. As the allies advanced people started to drift back and the Jews came out of hiding, but there were some that never returned. Our war wasn't ended. The first thing we wanted was revenge. Those girls who had fraternised with the Germans were fetched out first and their heads shaved and swastikas painted on their skulls. You felt sorry for them, we didn't. They got what they deserved. They couldn't be trusted, it was them who had betrayed secrets and the names of resistance workers to their German boyfriends. We captured all those Quislings and gave them a taste of their own medicine. We lined them up and marched them to the concentration camp and forced them to wear the striped uniforms that their victims had been made to wear. The resistance would have liked to deal with them, but the British military police took over.

The Germans had gone but they nearly came back in the Battle of Ardennes. That was terrible. We were all apprehensive and frightened in those months. There were the V1s and the V2s going overhead. There were four launch sites near Njimegen and they were aiming at London and Antwerp. Many of them aborted. Some exploded on Vught and several people were killed.

We were now thinking of our family. We were free but the north of the country was still in German hands and we knew that thousands were dying from starvation. We had no word from my sister and her family. They were freed on May 5th 1945. A friend and I took parcels and managed to get them through to Edam and found that they were still alive. It had been a difficult journey because the bridges had been bombed and there were many refugees on the road.

My sister and her family had been lucky, because they lived near the country, her husband had crept out during the night and stolen sugar beet from the fields. They even dug up the bulbs and ate those. They were also lucky because they had a little paraffin. Her husband was a teacher in a technical college and they had paraffin to heat the classrooms, but lessons were stopped, so the teachers divided the paraffin between themselves. That meant they could boil the sugar beet and they gave the liquid to the children. It kept them alive. One day my brother in law heard that a farmer had apples for sale and he walked nine kilometres to the farm and managed to get two apples. He said he was so hungry, he ate one and took the other home.

I thought my sister would be pleased to see us, but there was a feeling of resentment. She thought we should have got food to them but there was nothing we could have done. There was no doubt that they had suffered.

We had not heard from my brother in the navy either. Then in February he came home. He had ten days leave and had hitch hiked from Ostend. It was the first time he knew he had a daughter, four years old. He had known his wife was pregnant, when he left in 1940. I shall never forget his face when he saw his wife and daughter.

"I have a new daughter and a new wife," he said. But it wasn't easy for them, when he did return for good. They had been apart for five years and had experienced so many different things. They had to get to know each other again and that did not happen immediately, but they settled down alright. There were some who returned after such a long absence, who found they were married to strangers and they remained strangers and drifted apart.

We had such a party and we weren't the only ones celebrating the return of loved ones. My brother said we shouldn't see the Germans as our enemies when the war was over, Russia would be the problem. We knew who our enemies were, we had been forced to live with them for four and a half years.

I didn't need to think twice about my future. I joined the Dutch army as soon as I could.

Once Upon A Wartime III

Above: *Hubertus Lafaeber's Identity Card issued by the Germans*

Left: *Prisoners from Amersfoort walking from the station to Vught concentration camp through Helvoirtsweg*

Below: *Catharina Stacey at work in September 1943*

Once Upon A Wartime III

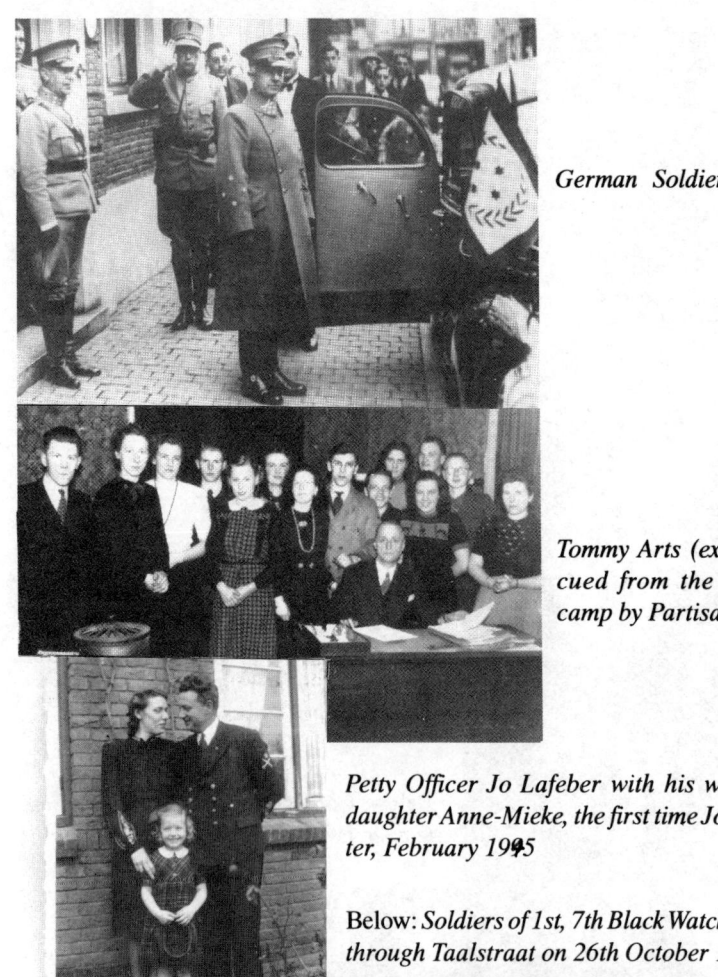

German Soldiers in Vught 1942

Tommy Arts (extreme left) rescued from the concentration camp by Partisans

Petty Officer Jo Lafeber with his wife Jeanne and daughter Anne-Mieke, the first time Jo met his daughter, February 1945

Below: *Soldiers of 1st, 7th Black Watch entering Vught through Taalstraat on 26th October 1944*

Once Upon A Wartime III

Operation Manna

I was brought up in a theatrical family. My father managed a theatre. I didn't really know what I wanted to do when I left school but I knew I didn't want to be an actor. I had had enough of that as a child. My father was one for publicity and special effects. When the talking films came in, he liked to have theatrical performances. He was always trying to work out new ideas. Forthcoming attractions were heralded by trailers which were shown during the interval. My father would have a gauze screen brought down during these trailers and actors acting a scene of the film to come. When he showed The Hunchback of Notredame, he found an actor who really was a hunchback. The hunchback came down a rope hand over hand and really did make a bell ring. Then he shambled across the stage and kicked a pile of rags. A girl sat up and when she saw the horrific face, she screamed. Well my father made it so realistic that he had to have nurses in the audience because so many people fainted.

Then there was the film with the two Gish sisters in it who rescued this child. He had the actors behind the same gauze curtain. I was the child. I didn't like the acting, but I was fascinated with the special effects and the lighting.

I was eighteen and getting ready to go to University when a friend showed me an advertisement in the newspaper for short service commissions in the RAF. It was a chance to learn to fly and I applied. Until then, Officer Cadets needed a degree before they trained, but the RAF had found themselves short of pilots and these short service commissions were for six years of service and four in the reserve. I was invited to an interview at Astra House in Kingsway and was accepted with the rank of Acting Pilot Officer. I reported to Uxbridge for my uniform and was then posted to Yatesbury in Wiltshire for EFTS (Elementary Flying Training School).

I didn't find it difficult to fit into mess life as I had been used to meeting people from all walks of life in the theatre. It took me some time to get used to all the protocol and correct procedures. One didn't wear uniform in town for example. I had my own batman in the mess so all I had to concentrate on was learning how to fly.

We learned to fly Tiger Moths. We had to do fifty hours, twenty-five under instruction and twenty-five solo. We took an exam at the end of the course and I was then transferred to Peterborough for SFTS (Service Flying Training School). We flew Hawker Harts there and there were two parts to the course, junior and senior. At the end of that course we were asked in which branch we would like to serve and I said Flying boats, but I didn't get them. Instead the instructor asked me if I had thought of becoming an instructor. That was the cream. Of course I hadn't thought of it, but they were short of pilots.

It was when I was in Peterborough that I saw an advertisement for the Seven Musical Elliots in the theatre there. I'd met them when they'd worked at my father's theatre, so I went round to the stage door and, to cut a long story short, I started seeing a lot of one of the daughters and our relationship became serious. I phoned her regularly and if you remember in the 1930s, trunk calls had to go through the operator and it reached the stage where he used to say to me, "Where is she this week then Sir?" They were a well known musical group and they appeared in theatres all over the country, in different parts of the world too.

I was now posted to Old Sarum, to the School of Army Co-operation and that was where I discovered we were scheduled for overseas posting at the end of the course and in fact, I left for India on Christmas Eve of 1938, but I was married before I went. It was a difficult situation because officers were not given permission to marry before they attained the rank of Squadron Leader or had reached the age of twenty-five. I could aspire to neither of those. I was still an acting pilot officer, but my fiancee was adamant, she wanted to be Mrs Butler before I went. Someone pointed out that the RAF could not stop me marrying. The only thing they could do was not give us any marriage allowances or quarters, so, with the help of the padre, we married at the local registry office and we had eight days and nine nights together before I sailed.

I had been posted to one of the RAF's oldest squadrons, the 28th, which was based at Ambala. After two months the unit was transferred to Kohat, thirty miles south of Peshawar, close to the north west frontier with Afganistan. Our job was to 'watch and ward' that frontier.

It was a mountainous and inhospitable land. It was a five day train journey to get there. I got to know the Khyber pass, I flew more hours over that than I had flown altogether in England. We were on constant watch over the north west frontier. King Amanallah had lost faith with the British protectorate and was trying to re-establish his power on the throne. The politicals were in power in India then and had been for nearly a century, ruled by the viceroy. Their intelligence system was efficient and we knew where we were likely to experience trouble.

I flew an Audax Hawker which was fitted with two Vickers guns which shot through the propellers. A gunner behind me had a backward firing Lewis on a scarfe ring. We were often shot at but their artillery was home made and, as long as they were aiming at us, we knew we would be alright. Nevertheless we were given plenty of instruction and training if we were forced down. We had bed rolls and emergency rations and we knew how to construct shelters. We even had a length of rope with a sack which we threw over the propellers and with pulling and running we would be able to restart the plane and we did do it - once. We were on one flight and I was firing my guns when they suddenly stopped. I tried to get the breach out while flying. The plane started to shake and the shaking grew more violent until it seemed we would be shaken to bits. I didn't think we would make it back to base, but we did and I found I had shot at my propeller, but I managed to land. I was a bit sharp to the armourers. I thought they had loaded up wrongly. The gun should have loaded itself but the pin that hit the cap had pierced it and jammed the whole thing up. The gunners made me a present of the prop and I've still got it. It was a relief to get back to base. We would have had an unfriendly reception if we'd been forced to land.

India at this time was divided into different states some of which were ruled by Royal families. Some of these families were very friendly and helpful to the British, but not all.

There was one occasion when some soldiers that had been sent up country were attacked and killed by Dacoits. The headman of the local village was told to bring the culprits in. The squadron flew over the village to remind them and we didn't fly at 1000 feet either. There was still no action so we flew over them again and dropped pamphlets. Then, after several more warnings, they were told to clear the village and we started punitive bombing.

By this time, war in Europe had been declared and I was a fully blown Flying Officer. It was difficult writing home because letters were censored. The Maharajah had contacted the viceroy and asked what he could do to help. He was a fully qualified pilot himself and he was made an honorary Air Commodore. He was invited to our air base for the day. We prepared for the visit in the usual RAF manner - if it moves salute it, if it doesn't pick it up and if you can't, whitewash it. The day finished with a dinner in the mess. Afterwards several of us went for a breath of fresh air and I found myself standing beside the Station Commander. He asked me how my family were and I told him that I didn't know when I would see my wife again. He told me he'd have a word to his adjutant in the morning.

The adjutant was most helpful and pointed out that India was still under Indian Government rule and not subject to the King's regulations. He suggested I got his babu (Indian writer) to check the regulations. There it was, any serving officer could apply for their next of kin to join them, at their own expense of course. The ruling had never been repealed.

My wife sailed from Southampton. She sent a cable to say she was sailing on her birthday, so I knew when she left. I was really worried when I heard the report that one of two passenger ships sailing through the Mediterranean had been sunk with considerable loss of life, because I thought she would be in the Mediterranean at that time. I got in touch with the authorities and Cooks and anyone else I could think of, to find out if she had been on one of the ships, but it was classified information. I just prayed that she was safe. I sent my bearer down to meet her. I couldn't have the leave to go myself. It was a five day train journey each way. Meanwhile I prepared the bungalow that was to be our home - which I hoped was to be our home. There had been a mix up with the quarters and we had been given a bungalow which looked as though it had come straight out of Hollywood, pillared entrance and all. My bearer had arranged for me to hire his brother while he was away. My bearer was Pathan, a big reliable man and so was his brother.

When I awoke from my Sunday siesta, he brought me a cup of tea and said, "Sir will be please to see the M'em. The M'em, Sahib be here for breakfast."

"How do you know?"

"Abdul phone from Rawpindi."

"Why didn't you tell me."

"Sahib sleep."

Rawpindi was only twelve hours away. My wife would be coming up on the overnight train. I had discovered by reading the regulations that we could hire RAF equipment, so I went and asked the CO if I could hire his car so I could go and meet my wife. He looked at me blankly for a few seconds, then he said "No. Certainly not." But then he added that his car would be there with his driver to take me down to the station. My colleagues had made a flag for it and what with one thing and another she had quite a welcome.

28 Squadron was to be rearmed with new planes - Lysanders. We travelled down to Karachi, which was five days by train to collect them. We were shown the hangar where the planes were waiting for us. There weren't any planes there, just huge packing boxes. They were the Lysanders. We had to wait for them to be constructed.

Mountbatten had been posted back to India for the purpose of creating South East Asia Command, preparing to fight the Japanese. One of the first things he did was to create a training force. I was posted to number 1 Flying Instructors School, Ambala on an instructors course.

Mountbatten's main ability was choosing the right man for the right job. He appointed Air Commodore Joe Vincent in charge of 227 group training and

I had the honour to serve under him.

The adjutant came in one day, but he kept his hat on and he saluted and handing me a slip of paper he said, "A signal for you, Sir."

"What are you playing at John?"

"Well read the bastard," he said.

I had been made the Squadron Commander. I was now a Squadron Leader. I was 24. We were preparing to put the air force into Burma. The Japanese would slow down when the monsoons started but that was when we planned to attack, only I missed it. I was posted back to England.

We came back by ship, my wife and our two children. As soon as we left port, all air crews were told to report to the gunnery officer. I took up my position with an Oerlikon gun on the starboard bridge. I had to pass the radar officer when I went to my position and one day I saw this spout of water that was shooting into the air, higher than the bridge. I had never seen anything like it. I thought it was a water spout. The radar officer said it was the remains of a freighter. There had been warnings in the night that there were Uboats in the vicinity so we had altered course and returned to the convoy in the morning. That freighter could have been us. I felt suddenly cold. The real meaning of war was in front of my eyes. We took several diversions to avoid Uboats and we spent five days out in the Atlantic before we made it into Liverpool. I was shocked by what I saw in England, the bombed buildings, the blackouts, the air raid shelters. We went to stay with my parents in Blackpool. It was different there.

I had to report to Astra House for an interview. I was greeted by the Personnel Officer, "Welcome back," he said. I was posted to bomber command to an advanced flying unit to update my flying. He asked me where I was living and said that I would be posted close to home. I went to Bauff. I flew Oxfords. I was a Squadron Leader, the same rank as the CO. My instructor was a Sergeant Pilot and I think he disliked the difference in our ranks. He was certainly aggrieved about something and after we found ourselves flying with a twenty foot view of the control tower, I suggested to the CO, that it was time he was posted to operational training.

I went on to Stafford and flew Wellingtons (wimpys), but it was in a Halifax that I had my first real experience of a sick aircraft. We finished our training with a bulls eye, a simulated bomber attack where we experienced searchlights, night fighters, the lot. We flew for an hour out over the Atlantic and then flew back in as if we were coming in on a bombing attack. We were flying over the sea when one of the engines started to race and we couldn't shut it down. It was difficult to keep the plane steady. Then another of the engines caught fire. Well the engineer managed to deal with that, but we were down to two engines and we couldn't feather the propeller on the engine that had raced out of control. I turned towards the coast and shortly afterwards, I saw a light. "I reckon that's Blackpool," the navigator said, "that's the only town that doesn't realise that there's a war on."

We put out a general distress call and Blackpool answered. We said that we needed to land. They said the air port was closed and they were under six feet of snow. We told them we had no choice, we were coming in.

We were soon over the air field. I circled jettisoning as much fuel as I could. They had the Drem system in operation and I was told to join the circuit at Angel 2000, that is at 2000 feet, one mile from the centre of the airfield. Then I followed the instructions to land and, as we came in, the undercarriage failed to come down and we tobogganed across that airfield, throwing up a spray of snow on either side of us. When we drew to a stop, all the crew climbed out and we didn't have a bruise between us. We all bent and kissed the ground. We were so relieved to land safely.

I was posted to 103 Squadron - Lancasters. I had to look after twenty aircraft and twenty crew. Each of the air craft had a name. The engineer came into my office and handed me a list of them.

"There's your family," he said. "Which one do you want?"

"What can you tell me about them?" I asked.

"Well, King is new, just in from Canada. Item is runner-up to Mike-Squared that has the DSO and bar and the DFC."

I had to get him to explain. He looked at me and asked, "Where have you been?"

"India," I told him.

"Oh."

Mike-Squared was an aircraft that had completed a hundred operations. Aircraft were awarded any of the medals that their own crew won. Every time a bomber flew a raid a bomb was painted on her fuselage, yellow for a day time raid and black for a night one. You trained with your own air crew and you stayed with them. You tended to become very close to each other. I know some of the pilots referred to their crews as family and it was something like that. I went out in the crew bus to look at the planes and the driver pointed out Item so I told him to go there so that I could take a look at it. As we drew up to it, the Flight Sergeant lined the ground crew up and stood them to attention. Then he put out his hand and, as you always do in that situation, I went to shake it, but he put his other hand over mine and looked up into my face and said, "She's a good bus, Sir. If you look after her she'll always look after you and bring you home safely."

Well what could I do after that, I flew Item.

We flew many operations together. There were just as many that were aborted. We would be lined up at the end of the runway and the red very light would go up.

As I say, the crew really got to know each other. The bomb aimer was a quiet man and when we were going back on the crew bus after one mission, I knocked his arm and he winced. I asked him if he was hurt and he insisted it was nothing, but I put my hand on his arm and it came away covered in blood. It wasn't until we got inside that we could see his arm. His whole sleeve had been shot away and a furrow of flesh the length of his arm had been cut out, but there were no bones broken and he reported for duty as usual the next day.

Bombing raids followed a similar pattern, the path finders would go in and drop flares on the target. It was often difficult for the bomb aimer to see where the bombs were to go because there would be so much smoke. A lone Lancaster known as the master bomber would be circling at 5000 feet and they would call us up and tell us where to drop our bombs, "Bomb the red T I (Target Indicator) we would be told. It was important that I kept the aircraft steady so that the bombs dropped square and that could be difficult at times when it was very windy or we were being attacked by fighters. This was why the armourers loaded the bombs so carefully so that they fell out in a particular sequence that would not put the plane off balance.

We all experienced the same conditions, the flak, the searchlights, the fighter attacks, but we had a job to do and we went ahead and did it. I suppose by sharing those conditions we did grow close. You soon learned to control your emotions. You couldn't let yourself think of those that didn't come back. You developed a kind of fatalism. If Him up there had decided to call you in, there was nothing you could do about it.

I was with 103 Squadron at Elsham Wolds and the CO informed me one day, that my plane had been loaded, not with bombs, but with sacks. I had to find out how they should be dropped. The armourers had fixed meat hooks to the bomb bays so that the sacks could be released like bombs. We practised and worked out that the safest way to drop them was from sixty feet, flying at a speed of ninety knots. We were preparing for Operation Manna. Queen Wilhelmina of the Netherlands had asked for help to save her people who were still under German occupation. They were starving.

The operation was aborted the first time. Harris refused to let us fly because he thought the bombers would be sitting ducks for the Germans to shoot down, but the Germans were instructed to stand clear and they did. The BBC put out an announcement the previous night and told the people to stand clear of the dropping zones. Then we flew in, us and the Americans, the American Eighth Air Force. Bomber Command called it Operation Manna, the Americans called it Chowhound and the Dutch called it (and still do) Food and Freedom.

We flew in and I lead them. Looking back now, I think it was the best thing I ever did in my life, but we didn't think so at the time. Well we had been trained to bomb, not take food parcels and we didn't appreciate the state to which the Dutch had been reduced. The weather was dreadful, wet and stormy.

The Pathfinders went in first, the same as they did on the bombing raid. My dropping zone was Rotterdam. The one person on a Lancaster who cannot see the ground beneath them is the pilot. Once the bombs have been dropped, I would get the instruction, 'Bombs away, head for home Skip' and it was the same that day. I banked to turn and that was when I saw the ground and there were thousands of people there, thousands of them, all standing with their arms in the air and written in large letters was the message, "Thank You Boys'.

What could you say. That message got to me. It still does today, but it isn't the only thing that is in my memory. There is a little girl in a red dress standing on a rise in the ground, but most of all it is the people, thousands of them standing there with their hands raised. We'd controlled our emotions on all those bombing raids, but there were a few tears that day. The men dropped their air crew rations, chocolates, cigarettes, anything they could find.

There were thirty three squadrons involved with Operation Manna, 3300 sorties were made and 12,000 tonnes of food was dropped.

It took me a long time to settle to civilian life after the war. I was tempted to stay in the RAF. I talked it over with my wife and she thought we had tempted providence enough. I settled into civilian life with difficulty, the excitement, the comradeship and, to some extent, the purpose had gone. I eventually found a selling job and that was how I spent my working life, but in all that time, I have thought about Operation Manna and been concerned that there is no memorial to it in this country. It was one of the greatest operations the RAF carried out. It was certainly **one of the best things I have ever done in my life.**

Ken Butler unveiled the memorial to Operation Manna at Elsham Wolds, North Lincolnshire on August 25th 1996.

Once Upon A Wartime III

Above: *The Memorial*

Left: *Group Captain Sheen paints on the DFC*

Below: *Sqn Leader Ken Butler in front of the Lancaster of the Memorial Flight*

Once Upon A Wartime III

Fleet Air Arm

I was eighteen in 1942 and that was the day I joined up. I went to the recruiting centre at Canal Street in Nottingham and joined the RAF. I had always wanted to fly, ever since I had seen a flying circus at the hundred acre field at Kelham ten years earlier. I passed the tests and the medical. Then the officer said that they would contact me in eighteen months time. That wasn't any good to me. I'd chucked my job to join the RAF and they didn't want me for eighteen months.

I must have looked dejected because there was a colour sergeant of the Marines there and he said, "What's the matter lad? Have you failed?"

I told him I'd passed alright, but they didn't want me for eighteen months and I'd given up my job the day before and I didn't know what to do. All I had ever wanted to do was to fly. I'd belonged to the Air Defence Corps in Grantham. I used to walk there from Newark for the meetings and as soon as I could I'd joined the Home Guard. We used to go and hold the Germans at bay down at Farndon every Friday night. Now it looked as though the war would be over before I had the chance to fly. I thought I had all the qualifications the RAF could want.

"You want to fly with the navy?" he said and took me across to the Navy desk and that was how I came to be in the Fleet Air Arm. I joined up as a TAG - a Telegraphist Air Gunner. Mind you I had to wait six months before I reported to them and it looked as though I was going to lose out on that as well.

It was 1942 and I'd got a job with Laings building the new runways at Swinderby while I was waiting to hear from the Fleet Air Arm. Then the letter came telling me to report to HMS Arthur at Skegness - it's Butlin's holiday camp now, but I expect there's a few people who can remember it as it was then. Well I took this letter to the manager and he said that I couldn't go. He said that the job I was doing was a reserved occupation and I wasn't allowed to give it up. I wrote to the office of the Fleet Air Arm and I don't know what they said to the manager, but he let me go straight away.

Half of the recruits at Skegness were university entrants and it was hard

18

graft. If it had been peace time we would have had to serve three years at sea before we became telegraphist air gunner. Now we had to do it all in eighteen months. We had to learn all the basic skills and discipline of the sailor as well as our own specialist subjects. I didn't find that too difficult. I'd always been interested in radio ever since my father had a crystal set. My father was an engineer and he liked anything like that. When I left school at fourteen, he'd got me a job with someone he knew who had a radio shop. I learned a lot there, not so much about radio but how other people lived. Dad had been an engineer at a brickyard and we had lived in a tied cottage so when he lost his job, we lost a home and we had to live in a sort of caravan alongside one of the old brickyards. After some time we were allocated a council house. I don't think many people can understand what luxury that was, a house with a garden and an indoor bathroom with a proper bath and toilet. I had to help fix the aerials in a lot of big houses. I had no idea that people lived in such luxury and had such beautiful gardens. I was always trying to peep through windows. The radio shop supplied electricity to shops in the town but the supplies were changing from DC to AC, so I moved on and worked for a garage in the week and a scrap yard at the weekends. My father had two jobs as well; you needed to if you were going to have any quality of life in the 1930s. Dad had been called up for war work at the outbreak of war. He managed the tugs on the River Trent at Newark. They were still steam in those days. I suppose I could have worked along with him, but I wanted to fly.

I got on with everyone, but I didn't make close friends. Well, it was difficult. Most of them came from a different background to me. A lot of the men had allowances sent from home and they could afford to bend their elbows with their friends each evening. I had to send money home each week so I didn't have any to spare. I spent most evenings studying. We had a written exam every two weeks and you weren't expected to fail. About two thirds of our course did fail - they had good educations but I was more of a technician, so it was easier for me.

There was one other recruit from a similar background to me. He came from Glasgow, but I didn't get on with him. I never had any money, but the others didn't make me feel awkward. Some of them had funny habits. There was one dark chap, who always washed with his scarf on.

I couldn't get home at weekends but a friend I'd made invited me home with him. His father was a director at Covent garden. The family always made me welcome.

It was the difference between the officers and us that made me feel inferior. It shouldn't have done, we were all fighting for the same thing and we all had to work together, but there was a tension between the ranks.

We had to learn navigation, signalling and morse - 22 words a minute.

Once Upon A Wartime III

We had to master eight radio sets as well as manage all the naval drill and bull. Discipline was strict and there was little time to relax. It was easier when we went on to air training. Many of the aeroplanes in which we trained had open cockpits, Swordfish, Sharks, as well as Proctors and Lysanders. There were three crew in each plane, the pilot, the observer and the TAG. We tended to fly in the same team and my pilot was a man called Abott, so of course everyone called him 'Bud' and he was a bit like a comedian. He was short and solid and dark. He was a Londoner. He never had any money and he was always trying to borrow from us and he was an officer. He reckoned he had to pay everyone elses mess bills.

We were stationed at Ballykelly for a while. We took over from Sunderlands on anti-submarine duty for a few weeks. Ballykelly is on the north coast of Ireland and there is a strip to the west that is in Southern Ireland so we had to go round the coast to get back to base but Bud got short of fuel and we had to cross the Irish land to get back. We were lucky no one shot at us. The engine was coughing as we went in to land and when we did touch ground, the undercarriage collapsed. When I got up the next morning I couldn't feel my right leg. I couldn't manage to cycle out to the plane, so I reported to sick bay. The MO looked at me. He insisted on calling an ambulance and putting me on a stretcher. I was taken to an American hospital where I was seen by a succession of American doctors who all wore fancy boots. They all had cigars drooping from the sides of their mouths and they didn't take them out to speak. They checked me over, one after the other and told me that I didn't have appendicitis. They didn't seem to know that I'd been in a crash. They gave me an enema. That cured me quickly and I went back to Ballykelly.

I had to keep off flying for a couple of weeks and the CO sent me down to Londonderry to keep me occupied. I was taken down by car and told to go through a door. I'd never seen so much gold braid in my life. There were about fifty of them sitting round a table. They were discussing the merchant navy. They had just come in from an Atlantic convoy and were discussing what had gone wrong and what improvements were needed. I felt really out of place, but there was no need. They treated me like an equal and I had lunch with them. It gave me an idea of what we were to see when we really got into the war.

Then we moved up to Scotland for specific training. We were flying Barracudas along the coast in Kintyre. We were stationed in Macrahinnish. We knew why we were being trained - to attack and sink the Tirpitz. The German battleship was hiding in a Norwegian fiord and Churchill wanted it out of action before the invasion.

We practised bombing the Tirpitz. We dropped four pairs of bombs, so we had to make four runs on the target. After we had dropped the fourth pair, we returned to base and Bud Abbot went over the headlands so low that we reckoned he was trying to cut the grass. One day he flew back over the headland near this farmhouse. There were these two ladies standing and talking. One of them threw herself down on the ground and the other ran, I don't know how he avoided them. Bud liked to fly low over the Wrens when they stood on the high land at the end of the inlet and marked where the 'bombs' had dropped. Bud liked the ladies, but he was sweet on one particular Wren. One day when we were going in to land, he spotted this Wren cycling round the perimeter, so he landed right in front of her and instead of shutting the engines down, he opened them up. I think that was the end of that friendship.

We were posted to HMS Victorious. I had a different pilot now as Bud had been sent back for more training. The pilots hated it when that happened. We followed the Russian convoys for a while hoping that would tempt the Tirpitz out but she stayed shut in the fiord. King George the Fifth and the Ansom went with the convoys the whole time looking out for her. Then it was decided that we would go in and attack.

The Tirpitz was in a fiord that was barely three times her own length. Midget submarines had attacked her the previous September and done some damage. We went in at two o'clock in the morning with all that we could carry. We got there before they could ignite a smoke screen. The first two squadrons caused damage. We went in on the second wave. The plane alongside us was hit and she crashed into the mountain going in on a dive. Our plane was rocked by the explosion but we didn't have time to spare a thought for the crew. We had to dive towards the Tirpitz, drop our bombs and make our way back to the ship independently.

We returned to base, then came out on the Victorious again in May. Well, we drew the short straw. It was May 5th 1944. We were sent up to spy out the land, or sea, whichever way you like to look at it. We hadn't been in the air for long when the mist came down, one of those mists that you get in the Arctic Circle, where everything is hidden. The mist had come down in seconds, we didn't even have time to check our positions. We were alone in the clear skies and beneath us the mist covered the whole world. We couldn't see a thing and we had left it too late to reach Sweden. There was an hour's flying to get back to the Victorious and there was no chance of finding her in that mist if we did fly there. We were running low on fuel so we turned towards the coast. We had to find somewhere to land. If you know that coast, you'll know it's not very hospitable, not for a plane that is fast running our of fuel. It's rocky mountainous. We made for some islands but even they were similar to the coast. We were flying low at this stage and the fuel gauge was hard on empty. We flew over Sonja but there was nowhere we could have landed there. We flew on to Andoya. There was an area of beach on the far end and the pilot managed to land on that. The engine was coughing as we landed. We only just made it. We had landed on gravelly sand. My first thought was to destroy the IFF (indicator friend or foe).

Once Upon A Wartime III

There were two buttons we could press and I was just about to press them when I thought, if it destroys the radio, it could destroy me as well, so I put the cover back over the switch and tried to manhandle the machine gun. It took some strength to do it but I managed to get it into position and I shot the radio out. Then I joined the other two on the beach. It was cold. I'd never experienced cold like it. There wasn't any snow but there was a wind blowing that cut into you.

There was a village called Stava not far away and a man came out to us from there but he didn't walk. He crawled through the sand dunes on his belly. We'd had lessons in Norwegian on board ship, so we could understand some of what he was saying. He said that there were no Germans in the village but there was a Quisling there, you know, someone who was in the German pay and he had already reported our landing. The man thought it would take them a couple of hours to reach us.

We set about destroying the aircraft. Then we walked towards the village. There was no one about. We didn't go to any of the houses. We didn't want to get any of them into trouble with the Germans and we knew there would be the Quisling watching us. We walked on and took shelter in a barn. It was such a relief to get out of that wind. We emptied out our pockets and sorted out our escape gear. We decided to get rid of the lot. We took some bricks out of the wall and hid everything we had in the cavity. Then we sat and waited.

We heard the noise of the engines and we watched the German scout cars roar past. They went to the plane first. Then they came to the barn. There were two motor bikes with side cars. Machine guns were mounted on the side cars and they pointed these at us. A German ordered us to stand up and they started to search us. The pilot first, the observer and then me. He felt down my body and then suddenly my heart missed a beat. I had a commando knife in my belt at the back and I had forgotten to remove it. The German had felt it. There was a lot of shouting and I was seized by the collar and my tunic was torn open and the knife was pulled out. At that moment there was a hail of bullets from one of the machine guns. The four of us threw ourselves on the ground. The German soldier stood up and started shouting and raving. A German scout car drove up at this point and a German officer got out. He was shown my commando knife. He snatched my helmet from my head and started to beat me around the head. All the time he was shouting at me, but I couldn't understand what he was saying. I tried to keep standing but I sunk to the ground, I was lifted on to my feet again and the officer went on beating me about the head. I was bleeding from my nose and mouth.

We were taken out from there and we were put into cars, each one of us in a different car. The officer came along and insisted that I got out of the car and he made me sit on the mudguard and that was how I travelled, in the cold. It was bitter cold. After a while, the car stopped and the Germans got me inside and I sat beside the soldier with the machine gun. The driver passed cigarettes round and there was one for me. The man next to me handed me the machine gun to hold so that he could search his pockets for matches.

They put us on a fishing boat and took us to the mainland. There we were transferred to a motor torpedo boat and taken to Tromso. That was where I was taken to Gestapo headquarters for questioning. The atmosphere in that place was dreadful. It was cold, stark and forbidding. No one smiled. The soldiers were all in their black uniforms with polished jack boots. Even the civilians wore black. I was terrified. I couldn't stop shaking, but I wasn't going to let the Gestapo see that I was frightened.

I was pushed into a room and told to sit at a table. I sat and waited. After a while the door opened and a man came in, if you could call him a man. He was bent over double so he had to lift his eyes towards the top of his head to look at me. There was this haunted look in his eyes. He was a prisoner, he wore the pyjama type clothes that prisoners wore. He slunk around the edge of the room, then darted forward and put an empty plate on the table in front of me. I spoke to him, almost as you would speak to a frightened puppy, I told him I was English. He was frightened because I had spoken to him. I can't describe the look on his face, but his eyes looked from side to side and he half ran, half shambled out of the room. It shook me up, seeing a human being reduced to that.

The Germans could speak English fluently. They started questioning me straight away and when they didn't get the answers they wanted, they beat me up, thumping me in the stomach and on the back. Then they would rest for a while and start roughing me up again. I gave my name, rank and number. That was all that was required by the Red Cross as I told them. I told them that if they carried on like they were doing, they would be punished when we won the war.

"Ha, ha, Ha," that was a great joke.

I was transferred to a catapult ship and put in a single cabin. It was warm and luxurious. I stripped off, climbed into bed and slept until midnight when I was shaken awake and ordered to come along. I would have been taken as I was, but I insisted on putting on my trousers and shirt. I was taken along the deck to a door. A voice shouted "Come in", and with a deal of clicking of heels, saluting and Heil Hitlers, I was thrust into the room and the door shut behind me.

An SS officer was writing at the desk. He didn't look up and I stood there trembling, partly from the cold and partly from fear.

"Sit down," he ordered but carried on writing, "I must take this information for the Red Cross," he said, "name, rank, number?"

I told him.

"Date of birth?" I didn't answer, I didn't have to answer any other questions. I could see he was getting cross. Then he asked what Hutchinson did. I told him that. There didn't seem any harm in telling him that Hutchinson was the observer, but I wasn't going to tell him anything else. He was getting madder and madder. Then he started on about the commando knife and said that I could be shot for carrying such a thing and, drawing out a pistol he jumped up and pressed it against the back of my neck. I expected that moment to be my last, but it wasn't. He carried on shouting and raving. I realised if he was going to shoot me, he would have already done so and that was the moment I started to get confident and annoyed at the way I was being treated.

I was taken back to my bunk. Then I heard Hutchinson's voice and I knew that I was not on my own. That gave me confidence. I don't know what happened to the pilot. We never saw him again.

The next morning we were taken out by motorboat to a sea plane, a Blom und Vorn. There were bench seats in it and Hutch and I sat down with a guard between us. We were not allowed to speak to each other. There were some guard officers on board and they didn't like having us with them. The plane was too heavy to take off and we had to travel a good way before we became airborne. We stopped at Bod to refuel and then on to Trondheim, where we were put on a train for Oslo.

It was the friendly approach there, "Ah Victor, how are you?" That sort of thing, but I still wasn't going to tell him anything except my name, rank and number. He took me along to the barber to have a shave and that barber cut me to pieces. I was a big joke. There were plenty of Germans around having a good laugh at my expense and I was determined that if there was one more cut, I was going to punch him but he must have got the message, because he finished quite quickly then.

I was held in a cell in the gatehouse to an airfield. I heard footsteps in the corridor and there was a knock on the door. I didn't bother to answer it. Then there was another knock and then another so I shouted, "Come in," and this Luftwaffe officer opened the door and came in. He was all friendliness. He had been educated at Cambridge and he was in the vicinity and heard there was an Englishman here and had called to see how I was getting on and was I satisfied. I told him I wasn't. I'd been there twenty four hours and hadn't had anything to eat. He went out into the corridor and shouted something and a hot meal was brought in. It must have been ready and waiting.

Before he left, he asked me if I would like to go out for a drive the next morning and he arranged to pick me up at ten o'clock. He did as well. He said he would like to take me to meet a friend who was keen to meet me. We drove to this big house and were shown in to a well furnished room. Coffee was brought in and cigarettes put beside me. Then his friend came in. He was another officer, but there was nothing smooth or friendly about him. He started barking questions at me. I was getting a feel for the language by this time but my Luftwaffe friend translated in friendly terms. It was the same story. He wanted information. I gave my name rank and number and refused to say any more. The 'friend' walked out and I noticed the coffee and cigarettes had disappeared too. I was taken back to camp. I don't think the friendly officer said a word to me.

We were taken by boat from Oslo Harbour to Holland and then on by train. We had the same guards with us that we'd had from the beginning and we were getting to know them quite well. They were pleased to be going back to Germany because it would give them a chance to see their families. One of them hadn't been home for seven years. He'd been held in a concentration camp before the war as a political prisoner. He was looking forward to seeing his family again.

"Please don't try and escape," he kept saying. He knew that if we did, he would probably never see them again.

We were on that train for days. The bombing was almost continuous at times and the railways were one of the targets, but I don't think the allies were too bothered about the passenger trains. We kept stopping. Sometimes the train would only go a few hundred yards before it stopped again. People would get off and go shopping. The guards did. They brought us cream cakes back once. We were quite comfortable. The train did not have corridors like they do nowadays and we had a compartment to ourselves. One of the guards taught me German and chess.

You must understand that I was keen to learn. I hadn't had any education to speak of. Children from my class didn't in the 1930s. I could read and write, but I didn't have the learning that the others had. That was the opportunity the navy gave me and I studied whenever I could. The C.O. had told me I was a "rum bugger" and I suppose I was. I'd taken my exams for a petty officer on board the Victorious and I was pretty sure I'd passed them so when I was asked my rank, I said Petty Officer.

We were taken to Hamburg, to the jail there. It seemed the only place standing. The city had been bombed to bits. It was difficult to believe anyone was still living in the place. I was put in a cell beneath the building. There were no lights in it. There was straw on the floor. I felt round the walls but there was nothing there, just a bucket and I knew what that was for. It had been used as well. The straw on the floor wasn't too clean either, but I found a space on the floor and sat down. I had no idea of time. Then the bombing started. It didn't seem to stop. I never thought I was going to get out of that alive. I was sure the jail would have been destroyed and even if I survived, nobody would have known I was down there. I thought I'd been shut away and forgotten. The ground shook with the bombing and the dust was dreadful. I lay on the floor to try and get beneath it, but even then I was coughing and retching with the dust.

Once Upon A Wartime III

Then the door was opened and I was taken upstairs again and our guards were waiting for us. I don't think I've ever been so pleased to see anyone.

We were back on the train then and being strafed continuously. We reached the terminus at Frankfurt am Main. There was a little wooden hut at the end of the platform and the guards put us on our honour to wait near there while they went for instructions. You must understand that we wore navy blue in the Fleet Air Arm so we weren't as conspicuous as other allied prisoners would have been.

We could see the toilets, so Hutch and I decided to use them while we had the chance. We were quite relaxed and we were chatting to each other. We suddenly realised a lot of men were standing round watching us do what we had to. When we got upstairs there was a big crowd standing around and they all seemed to be staring at us. We were still laughing and joking and the crowd started to grumble. That was when the ticket collector pushed his way through the crowd, shouting and brandishing a gun. He ordered us out in front of him, forcing the crowd back. Then he pushed us into the hut on the platform. The guards were relieved to find us when they returned. It turned out that allied prisoners had been seized from their guards and lynched by angry mobs like the one that had been collecting round us. That thought sobered us up.

We were taken to the interrogation camp at Wetzlar. All air crew were taken there. That was where we said goodbye to our guards. We were lined up and marched through the streets to the camp. I was standing next to a Jewish boy and he was quite seriously wounded, but nothing had been done to help him. He must have been in considerable pain, but no one looked at his wounds until he reached the camp. The streets were lined with people and guards stood every five yards. We started off and the crowds knocked hell out of us. There was one old man leaning on one of those walking sticks with lots of metal badges fastened on it. Well he took a shine to me and he started shouting and beating me with this tick. The guards didn't do anything to stop him. A lot of the other prisoners were being treated in the same way. I'd had enough of this old man so the next time his stick came down on my head, I caught hold of it and tossed it away. Suddenly I had such a blow on my back that I was bowled over. The guard had knocked me down.

I was sent on to Stalagluft VII at Banklau from the interrogation centre. There were forty of us there at first. It was a brand new camp and there were no facilities at first, just a couple of taps at each side of the compound. Sergeants or above in rank were not forced to work. We just had two parades a day. That was compulsory. The Red Cross sent books and sporting equipment.

I got on well there, I'd been one of the first to arrive and I spoke German and I'd been put in charge of a hut so the guards knew me. We knew what was happening in the war, because some of the men had made a radio, a crystal set.

It was January and it was cold and the Russians were advancing and they were advancing fast. We could hear machine gun fire at night and the Germans were getting jittery. We were all being marched out and were told to get ready. I was in the sick bay. I'd gone down with what they thought was diptheria, but if they were marching out, I wasn't going to be left behind. We were told that arrangements would be made for the sick, but we'd heard rumours about that before, so I marched. We were told that if any of us tried to escape, seven other prisoners would be shot.

We set off in the early hours of the morning when it was still dark, even the Russian artillery was silent. It was so cold, everything was frozen. Nobody had been able to shave for some days, because the water at the camp had been frozen and now beards froze like solid cardboard, making it difficult to speak. Any moisture from the eyes froze and blurred the sight. My ears and nose were numb.

We crossed the bridge over the River Oder. The guards appeared through the freezing mist like ghosts. We could see the wire protruding from holes in the road and we knew the Germans were ready to blow the bridge up. Even as we crossed the bridge in those circumstance I looked through the swirling mists at the moon's reflection on the frozen river and wondered at its beauty.

We had had a small piece of black bread before we left the camp and that was all we had to sustain us that day. All we could think about was a place to shelter with warmth and food. Your mind couldn't cope with anything else. I knew before the end of the first day, that I was not as fit as I thought. In addition, I had been give a pair of new boots in which to march and that had been a big mistake. Each step forward took an enormous effort.

Then an oxen drawn cart joined us. It was carrying several of the sick prisoners. By this time I was falling back, so I held on to the side of the cart and let it pull me forward. That night it was decided that the sick should try and find shelter while the others marched on. Someone had lifted me into the cart and we made our way to the village of Lossen. A civilian was leading the cart and he knew where to go. When we reached the Schloss we told him we were alright and he disappeared within seconds. We went through the deserted street to The Schloss. We could hear the Russian guns clearly then. The local priest came in and urged us to go to his house. I couldn't walk, so they fetched a garden gate and carried me across on that. We were given hot, watery soup and nuns came to dress our wounds. I shouted out when they started to cut my boots from my feet, but there was nothing else they could do. My feet were so swollen. Besides the soreness, part of my feet were frost bitten. They bandaged them and then tied the soles of the boots to the bottom of the bandages. The nun was grim faced as she treated me. She explained that they would all be shot if they were caught. I explained this to the others and one of the men went out to find somewhere we could go. He came back and said there was somewhere down the street. It was the old brewery and we went down into the cellar. There were all the old beer casks there and we managed to squeeze some beer from the dregs. Did it taste good!

The Russians went through in the night.

I don't think any of the soldiers were above sixteen and they were all like animals, no animal is the wrong word - but they weren't human. They all carried rifles and they used them. Nothing and no one was safe. They lived to fight and they fought. They were a good match for the young Nazis. They had been brought up to hate and these young Russians had seen what the Germans had done to their own country and people. Revenge and vengeance was etched on the face of every one of them.

There was an odd quiet about the place once they had gone through but others came after them.

We stayed in the beer cellar for several days. We were safe in the cellar. There wasn't any food, but food isn't a priority in a situation like that. We kept our heads down. The Russians were trigger happy and would shoot anything. They had to live off the land because they didn't have any supplies, so they would shoot the chickens, pigs, anything.

Some of the women from the village joined us. They had all been raped by the Russians. One woman had a daughter with her who was twelve or thirteen and she said that the Russians had not left her alone. One of the women had an ox cart so we decided to move. We said we would make for Odessa. We knew there was a British embassy there. One woman argued about what they were going to take on the cart. She wanted to load it with her furniture. She said it was her cart so she could put what she wanted on to it. I started out with them, but I soon decided to strike out on my own.

I don't know how I can describe the scenery - bleak, empty. Sometimes you would see other refugees. I was walking along this straight road and there was nothing there just frozen empty fields on either side and there was this figure walking in front of me.

I wasn't going very fast, not with my feet in the state they were in, but he was going even slower. As I drew closer, I saw he was a Russian soldier, so I kept back, well you never trusted them and they always had guns. He was staggering from one side of the road to the other. When I caught up with him, I saw that he was using a twisted stick for a crutch and that he was wounded. His uniform was wet with blood and he had a bloody bandage round his waist.

He was very young, only a boy, I doubt if he was even sixteen. I lifted his bandage to look at the wound and it started to bleed again. I didn't know what to do. We had to go on, there was nothing else to do and night was advancing. The soldier was almost too weak to walk although I supported him as best I could. The two of us staggered along that road, with the emptiness on either side of us. Everything was frozen, a white landscape against the dark sky. We walked by a wood and I saw a little hut under the trees. The door was shut, so I knocked on it. An old lady answered and invited us both in. There was nothing in there except two chairs and a table, but it was warm. We made the Russian as comfortable as we could in one of the chairs. The old lady brought us some watery soup. She kept apologising because she didn't have any bread. I left the Russian there. If anyone went by she would try and get help. She wanted me to shelter for the night, but I wanted to get on. She gave me a pair of boots before I left. They were much too large, but I could fit my bandaged feet into them. That made walking easier. It had been cold in the day but as night advanced it was bitter cold. I don't think there are any words to describe the intensity of that cold.

We had had plenty of instructions back on board ship about how to behave in these conditions and I remembered being told never to sit down in the snow, but I had to sit down and rest. I promised myself that it would only be for a few seconds and that I would not allow myself to doze off, but I must have done. I was aware that an ox cart was coming up the road. The man who was leading the ox came across to me and pushed me in the back until I stood up. Then he kept giving me these pushes on my back, making me go forward. He didn't let me stop or slow down. Somehow my strength came back and I turned round to tell him I was alright now and there was no one there! And what's more there never had been anyone there. The road stretched out behind me, lit by the moonlight. It was completely empty.

I walked on day after day. I met up with the others at Catacicci. They were all still together, although some of the women had left them. I went along with them for a while, but I was better on my own and I wanted to get home. That was all I could think about - home.

There was a Russian woman on point duty and she directed us into a camp, a work camp. I wasn't going to get caught up there. I stayed and had a meal with them, but I slipped under the wire when it was dark and got away. I met Hilde soon after that. She was a Polish girl who had managed to get home. She had been in forced labour in Germany where some British prisoners were working. She had some English which she had learned from them. Hilde took me home and I stayed for a while with her and her mother.

One morning I was picked up by the partisans, I'd been watching these people and it turned out they'd been watching me. They thought I was a member of the Russian secret police and they didn't know what to do with me when they found out I wasn't. They kept me shut in a room in the house where they had taken me. Later on they brought in a man who had been in the merchant navy and understood some English. He explained that it was unfortunate that I had been caught up like that but they were very sorry, but they would have to shoot me. There was nothing else they could do. He told me in such a matter of fact way, as if he was planning to walk down the road.

I told him there was no need for that. I could fight with them, but he explained that that wouldn't be any good. If the Russians caught me, they would have ways of making me talk and I would give their identities away. I tried to convince them that I wouldn't but he just shook his head.

I think that was one of the worst moments of the war. The Partisans were fanatics and were quite unpredictable. Concern would become threat in an instant and friendliness would turn to hatred. Life and death didn't mean anything to them. If it happened, it happened. The Partisans didn't seem to think like people.

They obviously had doubts about shooting me, because they let me go with them, but I was never allowed to be alone. I was always shepherded and often tied to one of them, so that I couldn't escape. Even when I went to sleep I was tied. I think I was more frightened of them, than I was of the Gestapo. They were ruthless. One day we went to attack a goods yard and a man shot at us. My shepherd took shelter and I was left alone for the first time, since I had fallen into their hands. I ran. I left that town as quickly as I could.

I started walking again and made my way to Cracow. There were lots of other refugees about, all trying to get home. I took shelter in a block of flats and met up with a group from Ukraine. They had contacts with someone who worked on the railway and he was going to let them know when a goods train was going in that direction, so I stayed with them.

That was how I reached Odessa, in a cattle truck. I approached the Embassy with such mixed emotions. I really felt on the road home, but the man behind the desk at the embassy didn't want to know. He gave me a ticket for the bath house. It was a communal bath house, manned by women. I felt so let down by the embassy's attitude, that I didn't know what to do. Anyway, I went for a bath and those women were great. They bathed me and helped me get rid of all the lice. I was covered in body lice. One of the women had taken all my clothes away and fumigated them, which was fine except that the process had shrunk them all. I felt cleaner and fresher, ready to face the world again. I wandered down to the harbour, the plan was already forming in my mind that I would have to make my own way to Port Said.

It's funny how these things happen, but the next few days are a complete blank in my mind and it's not caused by the passing of time. I suppose I felt so let down by the Embassy, that I shut the town and the experience out of my mind.

I can remember being hailed by two men on a boat and them inviting me on board. I can remember them giving me food. I can remember watching the lights of Constantinople as we passed. I don't know how I travelled or how long.

I can remember walking into the Navy House at Port Said and announcing to the Petty Officer behind the desk that I was reporting for duty, but I can't remember anything clearly between then and the time I left the British Embassy in Odessa. But then, you must remember that when I got back to England they tried to blot certain episodes out of my mind and something could have happened during that time that I don't want to remember.

The Petty Officer looked up at me and sniffed. He obviously thought I was an Arab. I couldn't have looked much like a serving sailor. I had an Air Force cap with no badge and the American pilot's jacket that the Germans had given me. I had my navy blue jumper and army trousers. I hadn't washed or shaved for days and I don't think I had eaten either.

"Who are you?" he said.

"Petty Officer Smythe reporting for duty," I repeated.

He told me to stay where I was and he went and fetched the duty officer. He asked the usual questions and once again I gave him my name, rank and number. They tried to verify what I had told them, but the Victorious was out in the Pacific and other than confirming that I had disappeared along the Norwegian coast and it was believed that I was taken prisoner, there was little more that they could say. I had no papers to prove who I was and they were very suspicious that a German was trying to adopt my identity and escape. Some of them tried that.

They looked after me and they gave me a meal, but I couldn't eat it. I crumbled two biscuits and ate those. I'd been so long without food that my stomach had shrunk to the size of a walnut. My story soon got round Port Said and a group of Wrens put on a party for me in a hotel at the end of the street. It was good of them but I couldn't join in. I couldn't eat anything. I did have a drink, but it tasted like vinegar. I just wasn't used to it.

There was a troopship out in the harbour and I was taken on to that. I was the only sailor on board. It was merchant navy you see and there were soldiers on it. I had my own cabin and settled in, but as soon as we set sail, the senior army officer sent for me and said that as I was a sailor, I was being put in charge of the six inch gun against the submarines. I told him I had never seen one. I was a flier, but that didn't seem to mean anything to him. I was to take the middle watch on the gun. I went and saw the soldiers who were there and they knew what they were doing. They didn't need me there. Still I did what I could. It was a bit hairy going past Crete because that was still in German hands and they used to send torpedo boats out to attack allied shipping, but we got past that alright. We had a lot of refugees on board, Italian and French mainly so we diverted to Naples for them to get off. Then we really started for home and I can't tell you how I felt. I was looking forward to seeing England with such mixed emotions. That was until I was told to report to a cabin. There were two civilians there behind a desk, MI5.

They questioned me. They wanted to know everything that had happened to me. They didn't have a clue about what it was like to fly or fight and what was more they didn't want to know. They had these preconceived ideas and that was that. They made me repeat certain things time and time again and then would pick me up if I altered a single detail. When I mentioned Russians going through the village and said they behaved like animals, the two men picked me up straight away. They told me that the Russians were our allies and I should remember that and, if I talked about them in that way, I could face a term in prison. I told them they couldn't imagine what they were like, unless they'd been there. They became threatening then. I told them about fighting with the partisans against the Russians. They were dreadful. They wanted to keep me imprisoned and return me to the Russians so that they could deal with me. I can tell you that I had been through many frightening experiences but it was those two British men that really put the fear of God into me. I think that interview is the worst experience I have ever had in the whole of my life. I felt unsettled and unsure for the rest of the voyage.

When we reached Liverpool, there was a naval officer waiting and he was the first one up the gangplank. He accompanied me from the ship. A rating looked after my kit bags, I had two, one with gifts I had bought in Egypt and the other with gifts I had received, mainly cigarettes. I still felt uneasy going down the gangplank. It was a wonderful feeling to land on English soil again, don't get me wrong, but I wondered if the navy would think in the same way as the MI5 men and want to hand me over to our Russian allies because I had been forced to fight with the Polish partisans. I knew what would happen to me if they had done. Just the thought scared me stiff and that fear stayed with me for months, years even.

I needn't have worried. I was taken to Navy House and given a meal but I couldn't eat it. I was getting better, but I still couldn't eat more that two or three mouthfuls at a time. I was kitted out with a new uniform and given a rail ticket home and I went straight away. They couldn't stop me. I wanted to get home. I suppose I should have waited until the morning like they wanted. I landed on Nottingham station at ten o'clock at night and the last train had gone. There was nothing for it, I had to sit there and wait for the milk train in the morning. Two airmen from Syston had missed their last train so I had company. The three of us reached Newark at four o'clock in the morning. The two airmen carried my kitbags for part of the way, but then they left me to go to their base. I got as far as the market square and I couldn't go any further. I was exhausted. I was so near home and I didn't have the strength to get there. A policeman came along after a bit and shone a torch in my face. He asked me where I'd come from.

"Russia," I told him.

He looked in my kit bags. I think he thought I'd been helping myself to a few things. Anyway he helped me round to the police station and I sat down on the bench. The sergeant started asking me questions. I don't think he really believed the story I was telling him. Then Jack Flowers came in. He was a detective I knew.

"Hello Vic," he said, "how are you getting on?"

They got a car and took me home. They'd had a telegram telling them I was on my way, but they hadn't expected me at four o'clock in the morning, I reckon I woke the whole road trying to rouse them. Then my mother looked out of the window and said calmly, "It's our Vic," as if I'd never been away.

I couldn't settle, it was great to see my family and fiancee again, but I couldn't eat and I couldn't sleep and I kept having these dreadful nightmares, mainly about fighting with the Polish partisans and the two MI5 men taking me back to the Russians. I think I reached the stage where I was frightened to go to sleep.

I had to report at Lee-on-Solent, to the air crew hospital. They tried to blot some of the memories from my mind, but some of the experiences were too ingrained. I began to eat better, but I still couldn't sleep. I used to sit in a chair at the window, night after night, watching the shipping going into Southampton. It was a busy seaway then.

There's a grand curved staircase at the hospital and one night I came to as I was running down it. I stopped and wondered what I was doing there. I'd got it into my mind that I wanted to see the sister, who had her office at the bottom, but I couldn't remember why. So I pulled myself together and returned to my room. There was a nurse lying on the ground beside my bed. That was why I had been going to fetch the sister. She returned to my room with me. I wanted to help, but she made me sit on my chair.

The next day, the doctor wanted to see me and he asked what had happened in the night, I told him about the nurse fainting. He asked me if I really thought that had happened and then told me that I had attacked the nurse. I had broken her jaw and she was badly bruised.

I felt dreadful, I wanted to go and apologise, but he said not to. He said that she was partly to blame, as she has come into my room where I had been dozing on my bed and she had shone a torch into my face and that was how I had reacted. And I couldn't remember a thing about it.

The doctor asked me questions about my personal life. When I told him that my fiancee was in the ATS, he said he thought it would be an idea if we married straight away. I was disturbed by the experiences I had had and I needed something solid on which to rebuild my life. He thought marriage would help.

Once Upon A Wartime III

We married on May 5th 1945. We lived with my mother at first. It was impossible to find a place of ones own. Then someone read of my wartime experiences and offered us a cottage at Farndon, two rooms upstairs and two down with the toilet down the garden. It was a place of our own. I needed to return to the hospital for treatment for another eleven months. I got a job in a garage at six pounds a week. That was good money in those days. I started painting again. I had been good at art at school and I became interested in photography but the hobby that took most of my time was collecting insectivorous plants. At one time I had the largest collection in the country. As I became more settled I did push the memories to the back of my mind, but I've never forgotten and I've never fully recovered from my experiences. I still have black days, bad memories and the worst of them all was when I came face to face with those two men from MI5. That was the worst moment of my life.

Once Upon A Wartime III

Vic Smythe 1945

Below: *6th October 1943*

Once Upon A Wartime III

Left: *Barracuda Mark 1*

Right: *Blom Vorn Float Plane*

Below: *Bombing the Tirpitz*

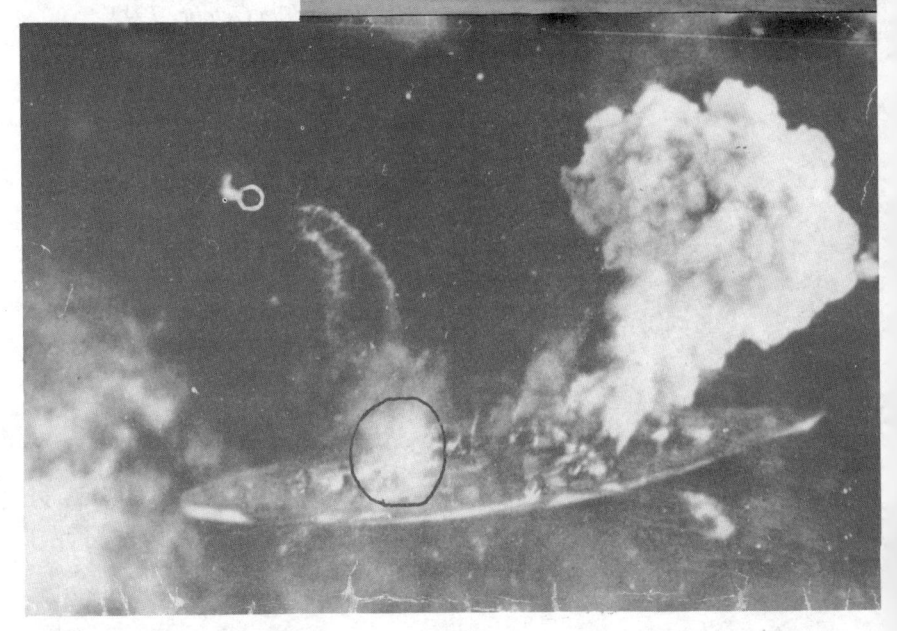

The Glider Pilot

I was born in 1912 in Australia, but we came home three years later. My mother was worried about her parents living in Hull with the Zeppelin raids and all. I've never been back, although I've plenty of relations over there. My Dad was Australian. I grew up thinking about the army. We were always playing soldiers when I was a kid. It seemed the natural thing to do to join up as soon as I was old enough. Mind you I'd tried working on the fishing boats first, but they weren't for me and as soon as I was eighteen I took the King's shilling.

I fancied the Household Cavalry but I wasn't tall enough. You had to be six foot to be accepted there. I was too heavy for the Hussars, so I went into the Royal Artillery and reported to Woolwich. Woolwich was an army town in those days, but we weren't allowed out into it until we had our uniforms and they weren't in too much of a hurry to provide us with them. I had been issued with essential kit when I first arrived. I can still 'feel' those towels after all these years. They were that hard. It was like trying to dry yourself with a wire brush.

I was put on fatigues until the squad was formed. There were thirty two in each barrack. We had been divided into two groups, gunners and drivers. The big blokes became the gunners. I was considered a big bloke. It was an endless round of square bashing and whip drill. We spent hours and hours on whip drill. There were four artillery groups, the light artillery, the heavy, the field and the coastal. I trained for the light. I also trained as a regimental clerk. I did a six month course in riding and horsemanship as well.

Then, in 1932, I was posted to India. We arrived in Quetta after five weeks on the troopship 'Lancashire'. It was an interesting trip on the ship, but India was fascinating. It was a wonderful experience to be a soldier in India in the 1930s. You were treated with respect and friendliness because of the colour of your skin. Mind you, you had to respect their ways and beliefs. The atmosphere could change in an instant if you upset them.

We joined the Second Mountain Battery, RA, the oldest battery in the regiment. It had been formed in 1749 as the Second Elephant Troop RA. I trained as a signaller there, with flags and in morse. I was in Quetta in May 1935 in the earthquake. That was a terrible business. We didn't have it too bad, mostly cracked buildings and a good shaking up, but the RAF camp was in bad shape and the centre of the city was devastated. Thousands were killed. I don't think they ever did decide exactly how many had died. We were sent straight down to help rescue the injured.

Later that year we moved to Razmak on the Afganistan border. It was rough country. We accompanied the political agent as he made his rounds of the hillside villages collecting rents and fines. We would be out on these trips for about ten days every month. In the winter there could be between four and six feet of snow and the day and night temperatures varied between forty five and fifty five degrees. We would have to climb anything from a few hundred feet to a few thousand feet to get the guns into action. We had nine mules to carry a gun, two of those had the ammunition. Ours was a 370 Howitzer and each mule carried a different section, the breach and trace, the pivot, the shields, the wheels or the axle. Once we were into position we could assemble it in thirty seconds.

We had the Johnny Ghurkas with us. I could tell you a lot about them. They made the finest soldiers. They used to set up sentry points on the hill tops to protect us from the Pathans. The Pathans would creep up and attack before we knew they were there. You would see these piles of white stones at intervals along the hill tops and the Ghurkas soon made those into butts, to provide shelter for themselves while they watched. Those stones must have been used for that purpose for centuries because as they finished, the low walls would be pushed over and the stones lay there waiting for the next man to come along and build them up again. Several times we found one of the Ghurkas lying with his throat cut. We marched 180 miles to Rawapindi which was our base for the next three years. We had plenty of adventures and I got my Indian medal. I was involved in the Frontier Operations fighting the Faquir of Ipi and his Pathans in the Khisora Valley.

In 1937 our unit was disbanded and we returned to England on the Troopship Dorset. I was given three months disembarkation leave. It was a bit difficult settling down in England after India. There was a lot of poverty in both countries, bad poverty but somehow it seemed so much worse over here. There were thousands unemployed. There weren't any jobs to be had. My parents had moved to Falmouth. My father worked in insurance for sailors and after a bit he found some work for me in that line of business on a commission basis. Then I got a temporary clerk's job in the old labour exchange in the town and they kept me on for a while.

I'd been out fishing off the rocks. I'd been out since early morning and I was ready for lunch, but I didn't get any. My mother came running through to the door as soon as she heard me and told me that I'd better get up to the office.

Once Upon A Wartime III

There was a telegram waiting there for me. I didn't stop to change. I went straight up as I was. The telegram was an order for me to report straight back to Sandown Racecourse, Esher.

That evening I was back in the army.

We slept on straw in the stables. We were kitted out with uniforms and the same rough towels. We marched miles and miles in those weeks and nobody would tell us what it was all about, but we knew we were getting ready for war.

I managed to get home for a few days and I got married by special licence. I must be fair to my wife. She didn't want to marry, not in a hurry like that, but we'd been engaged for over a year and I felt uneasy. I didn't know what the future held with all this talk of war. I wouldn't wait. So we were married and we had one night in the home we had been preparing and then I was back to the endless marching of the Surrey lanes.

On September 2nd, we were told to take our kit. We set off marching as usual but finished at the station and on to the trains. We went to Glasgow docks and embarked on the Reino del Pacifico and there we stayed. The Second World War was declared at 11 o'clock. At two minutes past eleven there was up anchors and we sailed.

No one would say where we were going. A week later we landed in Gibraltar.

I was part of a gun team for the first couple of months. There wasn't much to do. We kept a look out for submarines. They intended to protect the Rock. More and more men and more and more guns rolled in. New batteries were formed and I was promoted to bombadier and given a battery office to run.

The Royal Navy had commandeered a yacht, then they found the boilers had blown and they couldn't use it.. My office was on that. That was the life, that was. There was the CO on board with his batman, the pay clerk and our two assistants. The CO's batman was the cook and a darned good one and all. We started each day with a dip in the harbour. There was always a good breakfast waiting for us in the state room when we got back. The food was excellent, so was the company. There was a boat to get across to the mainland when we wanted a bit of life. If that was war, I was all for it.

There was some action when the French started coming across from Dakar and bombing us. The CO was wounded in the head and shoulder on one of these raids. When he came out of hospital, he was ordered home and he insisted that the pay clerk and myself went with him.

I was sorry to leave Gibraltar, but I was looking forward to seeing my wife. We'd only had one night together. I suppose that was the reason things were a bit tense between us. We hadn't had a chance to get to know each other.

I was posted to the Coast Artillery Training Centre at Plymouth. I was promoted to Sergeant responsible for the paperwork for three batteries. Plymouth was bombed dreadfully. People took to leaving the city at nights and camping out in the country side or in caves to escape bombing. We turned to on several nights helping to rescue people from the ruins. There were some dreadful scenes in Plymouth. That wasn't war as I'd expected it to be. Some of the sights sickened me. I wanted to pay those Germans back, murdering mothers and babies like that so I volunteered for RAF aircrew, but the CO refused to sign my application. He said I was more use where I was. I was sent on a course and promoted to Warrant Officer.

I was getting back to Falmouth whenever I could. I often couldn't let my wife know I was coming and I was right put out one day when I got home late and found a soldier sitting in front of my fire. He got up and left when I went in, said he was going down to the pub for a drink. My wife said he was one of her brother's friends and I didn't think much about it until I found him in the house again when I came home unexpectedly. I told my wife to get rid of him. I wasn't having him in my home but she said he'd been billeted on her and she couldn't do anything about it. I told her I didn't care about that. She was to get him out. I didn't see him again but I did find a strange razor in the bathroom one day and there were one or two other things like that I had to ask about.

Then the army were instructed that all applications for transfer flying duties must be sent to the War Office. So I applied again. Then I just had to wait.

In 1942 we were told that they had their full complement of aircrew but they were recruiting glider pilots. That is how I became one. I qualified at Tilshead. Then I failed my medical. I couldn't believe it. I'd never felt so fit and I hadn't had a day's illness and I'd failed my medical. I had a hernia. So did Cedric Birmingham. There were two of us, the fittest in the group and we both had hernias that we didn't know anything about.

While we were waiting to go into hospital, we reported to Brize Norton where we tested and delivered Horsa Gliders. We went all over the country with them. We certainly learned how to handle gliders in those weeks. We learned a few other 'tricks' as well. I learned a lot in the war that didn't have much to do with winning it.

It all started one Tuesday when the Tug Skipper (Flight Lieutenant Wilberforce) decided he was having engine trouble when we came abreast of Bassingbourne Airfield, so down we went. It was an American Airbase and were those Americans hospitable? They didn't have this concern about rank either, like they had in the RAF. It didn't worry them that I was an NCO, I ate in the Officers' Mess along with my pilot. Tuesdays was PX issue day at Bassingbourne and we were issued with our allowance of four hundred cigarettes and chocolates and some stockings for my wife. We also had the chance to buy alcohol and other goods at really cheap prices. There were things we could buy there that we hadn't seen in our shops since the outbreak of war. It was funny though. The skipper had forgotten what was worrying him about the engine when we returned to the craft and continued to Norfolk without any problems.

After that, we often had engine trouble. We could rely on a meal at the RAF bases and the occasional packet of cigarettes, but the skipper and I would have to eat in different messes because of the differences in rank and officers seemed to take an awful lot longer over their meals than the other ranks did. I would be hanging about waiting for the Skipper to come out and finish the journey. It was the American bases that made us the most welcome and were the most generous. I was able to send my wife parcels every week, mainly stockings and chocolates, but I could often send her luxury goods like underclothes and tinned goods. Those parcels meant a lot in those days, because food and clothes were strictly rationed and there was a lot of bartering going on. My wife could buy more with a pair of silk stockings than she could with money. It was about this time that her letters started to get really affectionate. I did miss her.

Then Cedric Birmingham and I had to report to Shaftesbury Military Hospital for our operations. I came round slowly. The radio was on and someone was reciting the first stanza of the Rubay of Omar Khayan and Cedric Birmingham in the next bed to me, carried on and repeated the rest of it, all five hundred and five verses, from memory. He had an incredible memory and a brilliant brain as well. He was always top of any course and he never took a note. He'd never had the opportunity of having the education that a man like that would be able to get today.

Then I was down to Stoney Cross to ferry RAF personnel and equipment. I missed D day. I had to go back into hospital again to repair the previous operation. There were a number of flops and aborted missions. Then I went to Greenham Common. We were being trained to land in the Champs Elysee in Paris. The idea was that a flight of 'B' squadron were to fly behind American Daks, but it was another aborted mission. General de Gaulle wouldn't have it, so we returned to Brize Norton loaded with goodies, (cigarettes, chocolates, sweets, meat, tinned fruits, stockings, etc).

Then it was Arnhem, Operation Market Garden.

Because of the Albermarle's shorter range, we took off from Manston in Kent. It was a beautiful day, clear skies, good visibility. There was the smell of new wood and glue that you always smelt in a glider and a sense of excitement and good humour. I was carrying a 75mm gun, a jeep and trailer, ammunition, a sergeant and three gunners. The trouble was that if it was good visibility for us, it was good visibility for the Germans. The barrage of flak was dreadful. Those that had gone in on the first wave had not met too much opposition, but we ran right into it. We were over Middlesburgh when we were hit. No one was hurt but the glider was in pretty poor shape. There were holes in the fuselage and the equipment. The aileron control wires and air pipes had been fractured, making most of the instruments including the airspeed indicator useless. That was serious. It was essential that I flew above stalling speed of 90mph. The tug pilot wanted to turn round and head back for England. He reckoned he could ditch us in the sea near the coast, but I wouldn't have that.

"If we can get to England, we can reach Arnhem," I told him.

I suppose we flew for another twenty minute, but it was difficult to control the glider and it began to sway. It wasn't too bad at first, a gentle swinging from side to side but it gradually became more violent until we were swinging from side to side the full length of the tow rope as if we were the weight on the end of the pendulum. Then the tow rope snapped.

I could control the glider better now that we were free of the plane, but it needed all my strength and concentration. It was landing that was the concern. I had no control over it. I hadn't any brakes - we had lost three bottles of compressed air when the pipes were fractured. The flaps were not working and I could not jettison the landing gear (the locking wires had not been removed). I knew if I didn't get the landing right, the equipment we were carrying would come through the front of the craft and we would go with it.

I aimed as best I could, towards an isolated farmhouse that was surrounded by fields and we made it, almost a perfect belly landing except that we ran into a wire fence I hadn't seen and the nose wheel broke off and came up through the cock pit. No one was hurt and we vacated the glider at full speed, but the Dutch had been quicker. There were thirty or forty of them. I think we were all taken aback by the welcome. We were hugged and kissed over and over again. We might have got ourselves organised a bit quicker if it hadn't been for that.

I wanted to get the glider unloaded but the metal runner troughs that the wheels should have run in were twisted and broken but Dutch brawn saw to that. They lifted the equipment out and we set to fitting up the gun.

That was when the Germans attacked. We hadn't seen them approaching so we were taken by surprise. We gave them a good fight, but we were surrounded and out numbered. Arthur Jones had been severely wounded and one of the gunners had taken a bullet through his face.

We put a white handkerchief up to surrender. Even then one of those Germans shot at us. His officer dealt with him though. The real German soldiers weren't bad. It was some of the youngsters you couldn't trust, the Nazis. They'd been brought up to hate.

They took the two wounded into the farm house and allowed me to go and speak to them before we left. We were marched off to Dordrecht and then POW camps. I finished up in Stalag Luft 7 at Bankau near Breslau.

I had one letter when I was a prisoner from my wife. I can't tell you how much pleasure that gave me, to see her writing on the envelope. It was contact with home. I carried that letter round inside my shirt for most of the day until I found a quiet spot, where I could sit down and read it in privacy and it was a Dear John letter. I think the bottom dropped out of my world that day. My wife had fallen in love with someone else and she thought I ought to know straight away, so that I didn't involve her in any plans I was likely to make.

It was the low point of my life. All through the war I'd made plans about the future and now they had all gone. It was a miserable existence in the camp and this letter felt as though it had torn my heart out. To be quite honest I don't think I ever got over it, not completely. It still hurts.

Well there were the endless days in the POW camp and the Black March. We marched 240 kilometres when the Russians advanced in temperatures down to -40 degrees centigrade on some nights. Then we were entrained for three days in cattle trucks (54 to a truck) and taken to Luckenwalde.

The Russians took the camp at the end of April 1945 but they wouldn't let us leave for another three weeks when the Americans collected us in their trucks and took us to Halle where they looked after us as only American can, good food, good beds and friendly people. I didn't mind being delayed there because of fog. Most of the men wanted to get home, but I had nothing to go back for. I had three days in a camp in Worthing, then three months leave on double rations. I was demobbed in December 1945 with paid leave until February 1946. I didn't want to go back to Falmouth. I didn't want to go back into the Civil Service. To be honest I didn't know what I did want.

I went back to my old job in the labour exchange. I was posted to Southampton and I was moved from town to town. When I was at Ascot a young girl stopped me and asked me where she could have a cup of coffee. She had come for an interview for a job and was too early. Well she got her job and I got a wife, although she was reluctant to marry for a while, because of the difference in our ages. I joined the RAF Volunteer Reserves. It was great to meet up with old comrades and the old way of life, even if it was only for a few weeks in the summer.

I went back to Arnhem in 1984, the fortieth anniversary and I visited Fijnaart where the glider landed. A man recognised me and fetched the dial sight I had thrown into a dyke along with the breech before the Germans captured us. "I knew you'd be back one day," he said. "I got it out of the dyke when the Germans had gone and kept it for you."

That is one of my most prized possession's.

I visited Arthur Jones' grave at Dinteloord. I had visited his step parents when I got back to England and found that he had died from his wounds four days after his capture. If you visit his grave, put a flower on it for me, a rose. He was very fond of roses.

Once Upon A Wartime III

Ron Watkinson was awarded the Distinguished Flying Medal in April 1946.

Below: *Taking off for Arnhem*

Sailor at War

I had never thought about doing anything else except join the navy. There wasn't anything else to do, not in the 1930s. There was so much unemployment, so much poverty. My Dad had been in the navy, been right through the First World War, the Dardanelles, the lot. He'd signed up when he was thirteen. He and his nine brothers had all signed up and gone into the navy at that age. All his brothers went on to run pubs in Portsmouth, not that we had much to do with them. My mother didn't approve of drink.

My father became Chief Petty Officer Stoker. All the ships in Portsmouth harbour were coal ships in those days. He used to give three puffs of black smoke when he was coming home and we would catch the bus and go down and meet him. We'd walk home and stop for fish and chips on the way.

When he'd finished his time in the navy, he became Chief Engineer on the Mauritania. They held the Blue Riband for the fastest crossing of the Atlantic. There was this French liner, the Normandy, always trying to beat them, but they never beat the Mauritania. Dad went game keeping for a while then, then he joined Customs and Excise in Somerset and stayed with them right through the Second World War.

I joined the navy when I was fourteen. I went to a training ship. My father had taken me to the recruiting offices at Bristol and I had taken all these tests there. There were over a hundred boys taking them but only three were accepted and I was one of the three. We had to report to barracks, HMS Drake. It was the first time I ever slept in a hammock. When we went downstairs to breakfast in the morning, there was a bucket full of boiled eggs put on the table in front of us. The boy next to me ate twelve of them right off! His name was Ian Harper, but we called him Eggy Harper after that. Then we went to HMS Impregnable, the training ship.

Discipline was strict. You didn't have a minute to yourself. Every morning at six o'clock we would assemble on deck and climb the mast. The Devil's Elbow was bent over so that you couldn't use your feet. You had to pull yourself up by your arms and you had to do it, regardless of the weather or temperature.

Once Upon A Wartime III

I've seen boys fall from the top. There was a steel net to stop them falling on to the deck but they could get really cut up on that net and, if they landed with their legs down and they slipped through the netting - well...

At the end of the year we had two months on the Isle of Man, then we were back to the mainland. Six of us were marched down to the quayside with our bags and hammocks and told to wait there for our ship to berth. We waited from three o'clock to seven the next morning when the Jupiter came in. Then we were allowed on board and directed down to the boys' Mess deck. I was just fifteen. There was a war on and I was in the navy.

I was paid six shillings a week but five shillings was slot money for my keep. When we went to sea our money went up to ten shillings a week. Four shillings of that was slot money, so we picked up six.

We boys were at everyone's beck and call and expected to do all sorts of jobs. Discipline was as tough as ever. I got six cuts for nothing really. One of my jobs was to make the tea, but I wasn't to pour it out until the chief came down. I waited for half an hour one day and he hadn't come and the tea was getting cold, so I poured it out. I got six cuts for that. I had to wear a white duck suit. They cleared the lower deck. If I'd had seven cuts I'd have passed out, but I didn't cry. It took six months for those weals to heal. We were at war and I was punished for pouring the tea in the wrong order.

There were three lots of double 4.7 guns on a destroyer. I worked on the forward gun. My job was to load the cordite. The shells weighed seventy pounds.

The Jupiter was on coastal patrol and we travelled along the French and German coast every night. There were some heavy seas. We were going towards Gibraltar through the Bay of Biscay and it was rough. I was sitting by the funnel with this Canadian sailor. We'd got friendly. We were sitting there talking and this wave came right over the port side and took him, washed him overboard. I didn't realise he'd gone for a few seconds. When I did, I started shouting 'Man Overboard'. At that moment all the lights went out of the sky. It was almost a haunted moment as if day had become instant night. We searched for over an hour. We had the searchlights on sweeping the sea, but nothing could have survived those waves.

We were after E-boats. We'd fire star shells to light up the area. We destroyed three.

I never did sleep in my hammock. You just laid down where and when you could to get some sleep. There were many times when I crawled into the ammunition lockers and fell asleep on the shells. I was so tired. You'd be out all night and then there was all the normal duties to do when you got back to the dock.

We bombarded Cherbourg after Dunkirk. We wanted the French fleet to come across to our side or give themselves up to a neutral state. We didn't want them to fall into the hands of the German navy. Two French ships had already come over and were moored at Davenport, The Paris and the Surcouf, which at that time was the biggest submarine in the world.

We escorted the fleet to the Mediterranean and were based at Gibraltar. It wasn't a comfortable base - we were so close to Spain and the Spaniards were reporting every move we made to the Germans. The German bombers and Stukas were the problem.

We were at Oran when the Nelson destroyed the French fleet. We'd given them five choices of action they could take, but they refused. The Nelson took five minutes to sink the French ships from twenty miles off. The noise of the guns was terrific. You went on hearing them for ages afterwards. Many of us suffered concussion. There's nothing like steel against steel. Those shells could tear holes in the side of a ship, bigger than this room. We went in and looked afterwards and we'd never seen anything like it. It was a mess of twisted and torn metal.

We slipped out of Gibraltar one night and bombarded the Italian fleet. That was hell fire in the truest sense of the word. We fired Star shells to light up the docks. They were all there, battleships, cruisers, the Rodney and the Nelson. Once they started up you couldn't hear yourself think. The noise and the flashes seemed to go on forever. I was in the wheel house. I'd just turned seventeen. It was a real test of strength to keep on course in a heavy sea.

They must have reported it on the wireless. When we returned to Gibraltar, the docks were lined with cheering, flag waving crowds.. The Captain ordered that we played martial music as we came in - I felt really proud to be British.

Then we transferred to convoy duties going out of Liverpool. There would be thirty, forty, sixty ships in a convoy and only four destroyers to guard them. It was the U boats and the Stukas that caused the trouble. Going out the ships were empty. We would have a rendezvous point half way across the ocean, then accompany the convoy back and the Germans would be waiting for us. If a tanker was carrying benzine and it was hit, the whole lot would explode and disappear within seconds. There wouldn't be a sign that it had ever existed. I've seen that happen. Then there were the poor devils that floundered in the black engine oil and you knew they wouldn't have a hope. They would have swallowed the stuff and got it in their lungs. We had nets over the side and sometimes some of the shipwrecked men would manage to clamber aboard. We tried to pick them up when we could, but we couldn't slow down. Our job was to guard the convoys.

Then we moved up to Aberdeen, going across to Iceland. It wasn't worth getting off the ship at Reykjavik. There was nothing there and all the shops were shut up. They didn't like us. We were part of the Russian run. We went to

Once Upon A Wartime III

Murmansk and Archangel. We weren't allowed ashore there. I doubt if we would have wanted to be. It was cold, bitter cold. We had to chip the ice off the guns and the deck to keep the ship afloat. The waves came over the deck and froze straight away. If we hadn't kept chipping the ice away, it would have destabilized the ship. You couldn't walk on deck. Even the ropes were frozen. Everything was frozen, the oil and the grease in the guns.

We went through the ice once. The sea was frozen over. The ice must have been 2" thick. It was that thick it lifted the ship right out of the water, then it would slam back down on the ice with such a crunch that it would split the ice as far as we could see.

The bows of our ship were filled with concrete. That had been done to ram U boats, but it paid off going through the ice fields. But it was bitter cold. It was warm down below and the boys' mess deck was above the boiler room so we were alright, but on deck it was bitter cold. If a ship was torpedoed, the men wouldn't have a chance. They would be dead as soon as they were submerged in the water, it was that cold. Their bodies used to float on the surface and we'd shoot them with .5 machine guns until they sank.

We found a German weather ship amongst the icebergs one day. Well we sank that and took the crew prisoners.

Food was difficult. Fresh food was a dream. There wasn't a refrigerated store. If we were at sea for any length of time food got short. That always seemed to happen on the Russian run. We had to survive on a tin of beans shared between five of us at one stage. There were shoals of fish in the sea, such large shoals that they were sometimes mistaken for submarines. When we put the echo finder in, dead fish would be blown to the surface, hundreds and hundreds of them, all sorts. We used to net those aboard. They made good eating.

We'd called in at Scapa Flow in May 1941, when we were ordered out. We were told, that if we were lucky we'd have a chance to meet the Hun. Night was coming in when we set out. It was a magnificent sight. The battleship, King George V went first, then the cruisers, then the destroyers.

We caught up with the other British ships in the Atlantic. They had cornered the Bismarck, the pride of the German navy, the largest battleship afloat, but there was nothing glorious about her when we caught sight of her. It seemed six Swordfish (biplanes) had dropped torpedoes on the German battleship and one of them had damaged her rudder, making it impossible to steer and now she was circling helplessly and the British fleet was descending on her, like bees round a honey pot. They were bombarding her. Her decks were in a dreadful state. Her guns had been so shot up, some of them were pointing towards the sky. Our job was to keep a look out for Uboats. Then the cruiser the Dorsetshire sent in a final torpedo, she was the only ship with any torpedoes left. They hit the Bismarck with three torpedoes and that was the end of the Bismarck. There weren't many survivors, about a hundred. The British ships started to pick up the German sailors, then there were reports of U boats and all ships returned to base immediately. There was no time to search for more survivors.

I felt really proud of our small part - sinking the Bismarck. She had sunk the Hood and my father had served on the Hood in the First World War.

We never returned to the Russian convoys. We sailed to Alexandria. There was a fleet club there. I met up with my brother Dennis, at Alexandria. He was serving on the Illustrious. They had been shot up and were sent to America to be refitted. They had a good time there.

Jupiter was on coastal patrol. Then we were through the Suez Canal and out to Singapore. Once we got to the Indian Ocean, it was really quiet. We were on our own. There wasn't any fear of submarines. We were kept at work mind you. We went into Calcutta. We were allowed ashore there, not that there was anything you wanted to go ashore for. I'd never seen such dirt and poverty. We went to a hotel and I got drunk. I was six hours adrift when I came to and I didn't know where I was. They'd stolen everything, my watch, my money and they'd tattooed my hands. I was that relieved when I got back to the dock to see the Jupiter out there but only just. They wouldn't have waited for me. I had to find a native with a boat who would get me out there, because I didn't have any money to pay them. I got out and climbed the ladder and there was the captain. I knew I'd be for it. Commander Thew his name was. I told him all that had happened and he just looked down at me and said, "I guess you've learned your lesson and those tattoos will always remind you."

He was a real gentleman but I guess he went down with the rest.

After that, it was Singapore. The Jupiter was in dry dock there. She needed to be patched up. We were billeted in hotels. That was great. There was the fleet club and Raffles. We had a good time in Singapore. We were served tea in the afternoons and we could sit on the balconies and watch couples dancing. It didn't seem as if there was a war on. We were only there a week. It was Pearl Harbour and the Jupiter was out of dock and we were at sea in a matter of hours. Our first port of call was Trincolamee, an island off India. We picked up Sikh soldiers and took them to Singapore. They were really packed in. We put awnings on the deck to keep the sun off them. They had many odd habits. They wore turbans and they believed that as man was born of man they would have everlasting life. They had this grease which they rubbed all over themselves, put it in some funny places and all, evil smelling stuff it was, made the whole ship smell. We were pleased when they got off.

Then we escorted the Queen Elizabeth through the Jahore straits from Singapore. She and the Queen Mary were used as troop carriers in the war. They carried 20,000 troops at a time. Well, we picked up a signal from the Japanese saying they had sunk a Chinese tanker and it was no time before we picked up this submarine on our azdic. There's no mistaking that signal. It's such a distinct one. Well it was immediate action stations. We dropped depth charges and up she came. The Jap submarine shot right up in the air, about forty feet, then settled on the surface. It was bigger than us. The Japs manned their guns. Our first gun fired at the submarine and they answered and that first shot went right through our gun turret and shot us to pieces. Some of the men were killed outright. Both of the gun layers were killed immediately. One had the top of his head blown off, the other was decapitated. Some were in a dreadful state. One of the boys, Jan (we always called them Jan when they came from Devon) had been hit in the stomach and he was on the deck, holding his guts in and crying, "I'm going to die, but don't tell my mummy." He kept calling out the same thing. Then he died. Our clothes had been blown off by the blast and we were covered in blood. I was so shocked, I just stood there. All I could hear for a while was the noise of the explosion in my head. All I could see was the men I worked with lying dead and injured around me. I was severely wounded. I had the fuse of the shell in my head, my wind pipe was cut and I was swallowing blood, spitting blood. The fuse was a spring. They had to cut from both sides to lift it out and there was no anaesthetic.

There were two uncapped cordite charges rolling round and I calmly picked them up and threw them overboard, I knew they could have caused trouble, then I ran down to the point 5s and started shouting for them to knock out the guns. They soon knocked off the Jap crews. I stayed with 5s and shouted at them again. All the time the Jupiter was firing at the sub until it sank.

Once we'd seen the Queen Elizabeth through to the Indian Ocean, we returned to Dutch Java. Those of us who were wounded were taken to hospital. I'd got this burn across my head and was peppered with lumps of shrapnel, about as big as my thumb nail, as well as the wounds to my neck and head. The man in the bed next to me had shrapnel in his lungs. They must have painted me with something after they removed what shrapnel they could (I've still got some in me to this day). When I woke the sheets were completely black.

The next morning the Captain turned up and spoke to each of us. Then he said to me, "Come on, I'm not leaving you here".

We were at Singapore the day it fell. We went in at night and it was as black as pitch. We went up the river and there were all these little boats coming down. They were trying to get out on anything they could find that floated. We couldn't see them. We could hear their screams as they tried to get out of our way, but there wasn't a thing we could do.

We went alongside the jetty and you couldn't see the ground for people. There were thousands there and they fought to get on board. We had to stop them. There were so many of them they'd have sunk the ship. We took some of them to Java but I don't reckon they could have done any better there. All the time there were the Jap planes attacking. They bombed the hell out of Singapore.

Then we were through to the Java Sea. The Japs had their whole fleet advancing to attack Java. There were our three destroyers and five Americans but the Americans got away. We didn't see much of them. We had torpedoes on the destroyers, five of each and we let off those at the Japs. We gave them everything we had. The Encounter was the first to go down. It was right in the middle of the Japanese fleet. When the smoke cleared we could see the sailors jumping into the sea as it went down. We had to get back to refuel and we were going at full speed. We'd been putting up a heavy smoke screen and that burned a lot of oil. We hit a mine. The ship was lifted right out of the water and then settled with a 40 degree list. I was on the bridge at the time and I ran down to the deck and back up to the bridge and the Captain told me not to panic. I wasn't panicking. I didn't know what to do. I knew it was serious.

The boats were lowered and the order went out, the wounded and the boys to the boats. I was the last one in our boat and then they said it was full, the wounded took up a lot of room you see, because they were laid down. When we got close to the shore we had to swim for it. I towed a wounded stoker along with me, Little Jan we called him. He was only a little chap but he'd been badly wounded. He was crying out for me to let him go, to let him die. He was in that much pain. I got him almost to the beach before he slipped from my grasp. He was washed up on the beach the next morning and perhaps it was a good thing he did die when you saw the extent of his injuries. There was nothing we could have done to help him. We dug a hole in the sand with our hands and buried him.

There were six of us on that beach and there was nothing to see except for the sea and the sand and the trees stretching out on either side of us, miles and miles of them. It was so quiet after the battle. We couldn't hear any sound of fighting. We couldn't see the Jupiter. We couldn't see anything, just the sand and the sea and trees.

We hadn't got anything at all, we didn't have any clothes except for the shorts we'd been wearing. We slept on the beach, only to confront the vast emptiness when we woke, the emptiness and the silence. I expected to see the other survivors from the Jupiter but there were none - even the sea was empty. We had an officer with us, Lieutenant Pirie of the RNVR. He went back to where the Jupiter had been but he said there wasn't a sign of it, neither was there a sign of any other survivors along the beach. That was the weirdest part of it all, that there was nobody else. We lit a fire and after a while four natives came out from the trees. They each had one of those big knives in their belts. Well, they shinned up these trees and dropped coconuts down. Then, they came down and slashed at the fruit with their knives and gave them to us and we drank the milk.

Once Upon A Wartime III

They told us to stay there and they would fetch help and sure enough a Dutch soldier arrived driving a jeep and took us back to Java and left us there. Everyone was aware of the Japanese threat and they were looking after themselves.

The six of us walked down a street. I spoke to a young girl and she invited us into her home. Her father was a doctor. We stayed with them for the night.

The next morning we made for the railway. We didn't have any money for a ticket, but no one was worrying about that. The train was packed and throughout the journey we were being bombed by the Japs. They must have stoked it up well because they kept it going. It didn't stop for anything. We went as far as we could and it stopped near a port and there was a boat in dock. We climbed off the train and just walked on board. It was an Australian Corvette. It turned out that the train had been the last before the Japanese invasion.

We went to Fremantle. I was taken straight to hospital. I don't know what happened to three of the others but when I came out there were two of the boys waiting. We still had no money and no clothes but people were very kind and took us in. Every morning I went down to the docks and asked the captains of the different ships where they were heading. We wanted to get back to England. Then the Queen Elizabeth came in and I went to see the Captain. They were going to Cape Town and we could go there with them. We got some clothes. A boy had given me an Australian sweatshirt and some trousers, but we still didn't have any money, but you didn't need any.

People took us in and fed us and the South Africans were so hospitable. If we were going to be stuck anywhere, Cape Town was a good place to be stuck. There was the Table Mountain behind us. I stayed with a lady in a bungalow on the lower slopes.

I took to seeing what ships had come in and going down to find out where they were going. Then one day this tramp steamer came in and they were going to Glasgow. It only went at five knots - we could have swum faster. That was how we got home. We got on a train at Glasgow. They never asked for tickets but the navy would have paid them the other end if they'd been awkward. The other two lived in Devon and they went home. It had taken us exactly eight months from the time the Jupiter had gone down.

I reported to HMS Drake and the man on the gate wouldn't believe my story. He wouldn't let me in. I gave them my number DJX 183691. They began to believe me then. I slept in a hammock that night. Then I was kitted out and sent on two weeks leave.

My mother was pleased to see me. She said, 'There's an envelope in that drawer saying you'd been lost at sea, but I didn't believe it."

After that I was posted to HMS Badsworth, a brand new hunt class destroyer. I went up to Newcastle and saw it commissioned. Then we were sent to the Mediterranean, escorting convoys for the eighth army, for the invasion of

North Africa. We were rushing troops along the coast when we hit a mine. The ship was lifted right out of the water and we were thrown up in the air as well. I broke my arm when I hit the deck. The mine damaged the propellers. No one was hurt though. We were just shaken up a bit. Just the stern sank, the rest stayed afloat. We managed to beach the craft and I just walked off it without getting my feet wet.

We were taken to the barracks at Algiers. I was a Leading Seaman by this time. I worked for a while with the dockyard police. You needed eyes in the back of your head to deal with those Arabs. They did the labouring jobs, unloading the ships and that sort of thing. We had to get the supplies to the troops but those Arabs would pinch anything. The goods were off loaded in big slings and every so often they would drop one and there would be smashed tins of beans and the like all over the ground. The Arabs would gather round and tuck into the spoilt food and you couldn't get them to move until it had all gone. One of them would get knocked over by the lorries leaving the port and in the time it took the driver to get out and see if the man was hurt and then get back in his cab, the whole of his lorry would have been emptied. But it was difficult to catch them. They were searched when they left the docks and they would be clean but the stuff still disappeared. We used to threaten them. I had a 4.5 revolver, one of those big, heavy ones, but you couldn't shoot them. I caught one of them red handed once, but he dived into the sea and swum like a fish. I suppose I should have shot him, but I couldn't bring myself to do it. I wasn't sorry to leave the docks and get back on board ship. I was on a fleet tanker this time bound for the invasion of Sicily. We were carrying diesel oil and we were to refuel the ships at sea to save them returning to North Africa. It was pitch dark when we set off and quiet too. We were part of a huge convoy.

I had six men under me by now and I had my own room and a nice bunk but somehow I couldn't settle. I had this feeling that something bad was about to happen. I got up and went up on bridge and the captain said, "What's the matter, can't you sleep?" I told him I wanted some fresh air and went back. I'd just climbed into my bunk when the torpedo hit us. The noise of the oil pouring out of the hold and the sea rushing in was terrific. Then it settled and we were still afloat. The oil was stored in compartments and only one was pierced. There was no fire. Diesel oil is too heavy to ignite easily, the flash point is too high. No one was killed. We limped back to Tobruk.

I was transferred to a cargo ship then but we had a different kind of cargo - German prisoners of war. We had to take them to Bizerta, further up the coast. They were in the holds and I had to check they were alright from time to time. They were real Nazis, arrogant Nazis. They were on about how superior the Germans were, even though they were in that state.

Then it was back to Sicily on a landing craft, getting the infantry on to the beaches. There was a lot of sniping. I jumped down into the water and my legs went from under me and I couldn't get back up. I've never felt so ill in my life. I walked to the MO's (Medical Officer). It seemed miles away and I had to walk through no man's land. I didn't have the strength to take cover and by that time I didn't care. There was a bit of sniping going on. I didn't know if they were aiming at me or not and I didn't care.

I had malaria. There were hundreds of soldiers there with malaria. They reckoned we'd caught it in Algeria. We were housed in these big marquees and given quinine. As soon as I had the strength I discharged myself from there. I knew there was a naval barracks at Catania so I walked there.

I served on an LST 42, a landing ship tank. They were big, 5,000 tons, capable of carrying fifty Sherman tanks or vehicles with ammunition. We went into Malta first. Malta had been bombed to bits. It looked like a huge bomb dump but the people had survived. They'd lived in these caves right under the rocks. Nothing could touch them there. Then we went into Salerno.

Salerno was hell - the noise, the flashes, the desperation of some of the men. There was no end of wounded. We took them off the beaches. They had the Red Cross people with them so we didn't have much to do with them but some of them were in a hell of a state.

We moved up near Naples, anchored off a little port called Positano. I wouldn't live there if you paid me. There was this volcano erupting the whole time we were there. You couldn't get away from sight or sound of it. It was worse than the noise of the guns. There was this sort of sulphur smell. It wasn't for me.

The Italian people were alright. They'd had enough of the war. They didn't want any more fighting. They used to invite us into their homes and offer us drinks, but they could be excitable. One of my jobs was to go into Naples to collect the post. One day the two men in there were having an argument. They were getting more and more excited when one of them took out a gun and shot the other one. He dropped dead at my feet. I soon got out of there.

Then we were loaded up for Anzio. We had to get in on a narrow sea. There were mountains on either side. We had driven the Germans off the port side but they held the starboard side. They had these huge guns in caves in the mountain side, which they used to run out on little railways. We had to go through that. The navy had stationed a cruiser there, the Penelope. We called it The Pepper Pot. Its sole job was to keep the German guns silent and fire at these guns when they came our of their shelters. She had nine six inch guns.

I was on deck one day, approaching Anzio when I saw this German plane coming over. It was really high. I saw this bomb dropping. The Penelope had seen it too and it was taking a zig zag course to avoid it. This bomb seemed to chase it, and dropped down its funnel and that was the end of the Penelope.

That was the first radio bomb. They sunk three ships in half an hour, but we soon got the measure of the radio frequencies and they changed them so that the bombs dropped into the sea.

Then we returned to Southampton. Southampton has been bombed to pieces. It looked like another Malta, not that we saw anything of it. We were confined to ship. We were not allowed ashore. There were hundreds of ships in Southampton. One evening we went in and these Yankee lorries were driven on board each one of them loaded up with ammunition.

There can never be a sight like that again. D-Day, June 6th 1944. In all of history, in all of the time to come, there can never be anything to resemble D-Day, June 6th 1944. I tell you, if I'd been a Jerry and I'd looked out over the Channel that morning and seen that lot coming, I'd have turned and run.

We'd set out in the night and it was rough. We sailors found it rough. As the dawn came up there was this scene spread out in front of us which can never be seen again. Then it started. There were 1,500 Royal Navy ships in position and they started their bombardment and they were bombarding the hell out of them. There were the rocket ships as well. The noise, I can't describe the noise or the flashes either. It was non stop.

There were 5000 ships on the invasion all loaded up with men and all going one way. You couldn't see the horizon. All you could see, whichever way you looked was boats. The organisation was brilliant. There was not a single collision on D-Day. There were all those craft and every one of them did their job.

We went into Juno beach but the troops had gone in before us and were well inland by the time we beached. We ran right on to the beach and the lorries were able to drive off without getting their wheels wet. The engineers had laid a metal road across the sand so the lorries were well on the way by the time I had a chance to look at the beach. My job was to drop the sheet anchors at the rear of the boat, so that we could pull ourselves off using them. We had two donkey winches, one on each side which pulled up the anchor. It was when they were in place that I had a chance to look at the scene of the landings that had taken place only those few hours before.

There was the debris that one would expect, the broken down jeeps, the hedgehogs that had had the mines attached lined along the shore line, but the thing I will always remember was the sight of the two dead men, one British, one German. The British soldier had bayoneted the German and I guess he had shot his attacker but the two of them were stood upright in death as if they were statues. The sight of those two bodies dominated the scene for me. I kept looking at them. I couldn't believe they were both dead. Meanwhile the business of landing an army was going on around them with clockwork precision.

I saw the tugs towing in the first two sections of the Mulberry harbour.

That was a fantastic invention. They would pump water into each sections and it would sink. Then they could pump water out and it would float. It could lift up a whole ship as if it were in dry dock. I'd never seen anything like it.

We were stationed at Tilbury docks, doing regular runs across the channel but once we had captured Antwerp there wasn't so much for us to do. Tilbury suited me. We could get ashore and go to Ilford. That was alright in those days.

Then I had the softest mission that any sailor could have had in the war, to return Prince Badouin's yacht to Antwerp and it was some yacht. It was luxurious. It has been in dry dock throughout the war. We had a skeleton crew to take it back. When we reached Antwerp, I reported to the harbour master and he showed us where to moor. There was a lot of interest in it. All sorts of people came to look at it. We stayed there a week and then came back on a destroyer.

I went to HMS Defiance when I got back from Antwerp. That was the torpedo school. The torpedo men were brilliant. They were trained to manage electrics in the whole ships as well as the torpedoes. There were about fifty Wrens on board seeing to the paperwork mostly and I fell for one of them. I'd been sent to teach them boat pulling, not rowing, boat pulling and she was in my class. We went out together. I'd really fallen for her and I asked her to marry me. She said she'd have to ask her mother so she went home that weekend to see what her mother thought about it.

It seemed her mother didn't think about it all. She didn't think we should marry. She was a Jewess. I hadn't realised that. Her family were Jewish and they didn't approve of her marrying a Gentile, not that religion was important to me.

I was disappointed so I went out and bought a motor bike. Well it was a twelve and a half mile walk from Bridgewater to my home at East Quantocks Head. I took her home to meet my parents that first weekend that I had the bike. We were nearly there when this car came out of a garage, drove straight out and we went right into it. She was thrown clear and wasn't hurt, but I was knocked unconscious. I didn't come round for two months. It was eighteen months before I was fit enough to leave hospital and by then everything was over. VE day had gone, VJ day had gone. The war was over and so was my romance. She never came to visit me and she never wrote.

I was sent to Chumleigh Castle in Cheshire, the naval hospital. Most of the men there were hostilities only, that is they had only joined the navy during the war. There were some cases there. The man opposite me had lost both his legs and both his arms and he was as chirpy as a cockney sparrow. His wife and mother came to see him and they started crying and wailing when they saw the state he was in, but he wouldn't let them depress him.

I made a full recovery and I returned to Defiance and passed out as a Sub Lieutenant. I was posted to HMS Trigg, the barracks at Davenport. I never served on a ship again, never went abroad again. It was a different world, a different navy. I had six years when I had had to be alert and watchful every second of the day now I had to work to try and make the sailors beneath me look alert. They were all national service men, completing their two years compulsory training. I had to train them and they were hard work. They were not interested in war or the navy. They just wanted to get their two years over and get back to civilian life. The war was already a piece of history and we could see that history being broken up and destroyed in front of us. They were bringing ships in and breaking them up by the thousand, beautiful ships that had nothing wrong with them, cruisers, battleships, destroyers, thousands of them.

I stayed on in the navy. I finished my time as Lieutenant Commander. I was worse off as an officer than I had been as a sailor. We had these mess bills to pay and if there was a mess party we had to pay our share. We weren't given the chance of saying whether we wanted to or not. I did 27 years all told, signed for twelve years, then ten. Your service doesn't count until your eighteen.

I went into Customs and Excise when I came out. I was married by this time and Peter had been born. I worked by Southwark Bridge and six months of working in an office was enough for me. I gave that up and went and got a job as a gamekeeper on Lord Cowdray's estate. We had this cottage in the middle of the woods with an acre of garden. It was idyllic. It gave me peace and quiet and time to think.

I went on from there to be head keeper at Aberdon Park, Lord Hilton's estate, then on to Sir Vivian Naylor's home in Clwyd and then I came to Easton with Sir Hugh Chumleigh. He was a lovely man. He'd been in the army. We used to go drinking together. We had twelve happy years there. It wasn't the same when he died and his son took over. I moved, up to Westmorland. That was an estate! We got 1,500 pheasants in one day there in four drives.

I was the first to incubate pheasants. We used to use broody hens until then and that was a dance but fowl pest had come in. We were paid £1 a head for every fowl we produced. We made a good deal of money out of that. They would pay up for moorhen, hens we'd dug up and thrown back on the pile, anything. Incubation was so successful, I started up on my own. We bought this 35 acre farm at Wennington. There was a river running through it with salmon and sea trout. That was the start of the Lancashire Game farm and it did really well, but then my wife was taken ill and she wanted to come back to this part of the world. She'd been born here you see and that's where she died.

Once Upon A Wartime III

HMS Jupiter

The Infantry

I left school when I was 14 and went to work for a pork butchers. I left there in 1940 and got a job with Dewhursts and on April 1st 1943, I was called up. There had been instructions on the wireless and in the papers telling men whose birthdays were between certain dates to report to the labour exchange. In 1943 it was my turn. My brother had already gone. We had to report on a Saturday morning. The next thing I had was instructions to report to St John's Hall for my medical for the navy. I had my medical and then they told me I was going into the army. I had my calling up papers and reported to the Infantry Training. I was posted to the South Stafford and reported to Hythe. We trained on the beaches and roughs there. I volunteered for the assault course and was posted to Dover. We could see the clock face at Calais on a clear day from our barracks in Dover. They could see ours as well, because the Germans would shell us. There were two kinds of sirens in use at Dover, one to warn of air raids and the other to warn of shelling. The civilians didn't take much notice of the first one, but the streets emptied in seconds when the other warning went. We moved down into the caves for shelter. There was one chap we used to have a lot of trouble waking up, he was too fond of his bed to get out of it, but this night we had tipped him out and he had come down with us and it was as well he did, because this shell came right through the roof, right through his bed and took the whole lot down to the floor below. That was the night a shell hit the front of the shelter. We didn't know a thing about it, not till they started carrying the injured back. Those caves were so deep underneath the cliffs that you had no idea what was going on outside.

We were moved to Grays near Tibury and slept in bell tents, 13 seams and 13 men to a bell tent. Then we were out on a landing ship tank making for the Channel. Nobody told us where we were going but we had a good idea, I didn't care. I had never been on a ship before and I was sea sick. All I could think about was getting off the thing, but it wasn't much better when we did. We had to get down the scrambling nets and into the landing craft. It was getting light then but that didn't help. The sea was rough and the landing craft was heaving up and down on the waves, the sailors were finding it hard to keep it close in. We had to jump for it. That didn't do anything to help the sea sickness. The others were just as bad as me. We were all wishing the craft would sink and take us with it. Everything else seemed to be happening in a kind of haze. The endless drone of aeroplanes flying overhead, the smoke, the smell and the noise. You couldn't get away from the noise.

Then the ramps were down and we were running up on to the beach. The debris and carnage left by those who had gone before us was spread across the beach. That was Arromarche.

I suppose because I was a butcher the sight of death didn't affect me as much as it did some of the others. We saw plenty of dead lying on the beaches on D-day and we had to make our way through them. We had our orders, make our way across the beach and get to Bayeux. You didn't think of anything else. You didn't stop to help the wounded. Someone else had been trained to do that. You knew what you had been trained to do and you followed instructions.

We re-grouped at Bayeux, then we fought, house to house fighting towards Caen. We dug in the woods outside the city, Suicide Wood the troops called it. Then we moved in closer to Caen and we dug in overlooking the city. We could see the Germans digging in from where we were. On the Friday night the bombing started. The sky was black with the bombers coming in. We were so close that we thought we were going to be bombed. We were deafened by the noise of the Ack-ack guns.

We went in at first light on the Saturday. The city was virtually flattened and you didn't think there could be anywhere for the Germans to hide, but there was. They had snipers in every vantage point. In places it was more than house to house fighting. It was hand to hand. We re-grouped in the evening, those of us that were left. The whole company had almost been wiped out at Caen.

On Sunday morning jeeps and trailers went round collecting the dead. German prisoners of War had dug the graves. There were dozens and dozens of padres giving the men a Christian burial, collecting their dog tags and any personal property.

We went on to Villars Briarge. The fighting there was every bit as bad as Caen. We had been given our orders. 'A' company was to take this farmhouse and when we had taken it, we dug in and waited for our next instructions.

Then we were sent to Benny's Ridge. Reinforcements were sent up then. They hadn't been in the fighting line before. They'd come right out of England. We had to clear the Germans out who were holding our advance across the River Orme so they came right into the thick of it. Digging his slit trench alongside me was Leonard Birch. We'd sat next to each other in school. Now we were back next to each other again, but in rather different circumstances.

Then it was the Falaise Gap. You've heard all about that. Well, we were the cork in the bottle. There were Americans on one side and the Canadians on the other and us Infantry held the centre and we were told to hold it at all costs. And we did. The blood wagons were out in full force at Falaise, but that was the beginning of the end for the Germans.

We didn't have enough men left to make a battalion after Falaise so we were disbanded and sent to other regiments. I went to the Queens 7th Armoured division, the Desert Rats.

We liberated Ghent. We had a welcome there. It was difficult to get through the streets with all the people singing and dancing and kissing and the like. Our job was to push on but we were held up in Ghent. We had to stay in a factory there for a week, waiting for supplies to catch up with us.

Then we were on the move again. We had to set up a mock attack, draw the Germans off so that another company could advance. That was when I was wounded, a bullet took my eyebrow off. The officer patched it up with his first aid kit and I went on fighting. We joined up with the Americans at Njimegen and there was some fierce fighting to get there. We saw the gliders going over in their hundreds to Arnhem but we couldn't get in to help them, poor devils. We used the gliders to make sides for the jeeps. Winter was coming on and they gave us some protection and we needed it.

It was one of the coldest winters I can remember. I spent my 20th birthday dug in the woods near Wehr. We lived in dugouts but we had made ourselves pretty comfortable. We had requisitioned stoves from the houses and you could see all these chimneys sticking out of the ground, belching smoke when we were in residence. We used to do two hours on duty and four hours off and we would wrap our feet with everything we could, straw, newspapers, anything to protect them from the cold. We could hear the German tanks at Wehr but we couldn't find any, yet every night we could hear them moving. They sent out patrol after patrol to look for them. Then they found a loudspeaker amongst the trees transmitting the sounds.

Supplies got very short. We were almost out of ammunition at one point and food was short. We were down to a tin of M and V between two of us for a day's ration.

The Jerries broke through at the Ardennes, pushed right back to the Siegried Line. I was wounded a second time there. I was shot in the head. I was loaded into a jeep. You could get three stretchers on a jeep and taken back to a first aid post but it took them three days to get me back to the hospital in Bruges. I was there for three weeks and then I had seven days home leave. It felt strange going home away from all the noise and fighting. I was walking down the road when there was this bang and I was over the wall and lying flat on someone's lawn in seconds. I reacted like that without thinking.

They could treat wounds OK, but it was the other problems that were hard. One of the men went down with shell shock. He fought all the way through to Germany and he went down with shell shock and went berserk. They had to tie him to the stretcher before they could take him back. He was in hospital for three weeks and then he came back. They said he was cured but the first time a gun went off, he was as bad as he'd ever been. There was another man who was shell shocked, but he should never have been in the army, he was far too gentle. They had to pump him so full of sedatives, it could have killed him.

They crossed the Rhine on Friday. I rejoined my unit on the Saturday. We would have gone into Hamburg but they declared it an open city. The officer told the major that if they did not allow us access through the city they would bomb it, so the Germans cleared the mines off the bridges and lead us through the town and, when we got to the outskirts we started fighting again.

We fought one objective, but we didn't hang around. Others cleared up the mess. We went onto the next. As we got further into Germany so we became hampered by the refugees and displaced persons, hundreds and hundreds of them pulling those four wheeled trolleys containing their possessions. You couldn't feel sorry for them, you didn't have time to stop and see if they were genuine. Some of the German soldiers had stripped off their uniforms and dressed up as refugees. You couldn't trust anyone. So when these four airmen came out of the woods and told us they'd got out of a POW camp, we were suspicious of them. They were wearing British uniforms but so had others who had tried to get our help and they had been no more British than the Queen of Sheba. We had been working our way up the hedgerows looking out for snipers when the men came out of the trees. Belsen, we had never heard of Belsen but after that day we were never going to forget it. They told us they were in a POW camp about four kilometres from the main camp. Well we'd never moved so quickly. We forgot caution. The airmen had convinced us they really were our men and there were others up the road. Well the cheers when we went round the corner with our guns at the ready because we hadn't known what to expect, they must have heard them in Berlin. They were climbing up the wire, trying to reach out to touch us. They were calling out for news, wanting to know if anyone came from their home towns. Some of them wanted to get straight back into the war and carry on fighting. Others wanted to get home.

Other units had come up by then who were better able to deal with problems. The padre wanted to get down to the main camp and I drove him down in the jeep.

Neither of us were prepared for what we saw. There were bodies, piles of bodies, emaciated bodies and others that should have been bodies standing there staring at us as if they couldn't understand what was happening and the stench, we couldn't get it out of our nostrils for days. We didn't stay long. We couldn't stomach it but when we came away we both knew what we had been fighting for. By this time I was hardened to death. It meant nothing. Suffering was another matter. We had to fight to make the world a better place than what we had seen at Belsen.

I was at Luneburg Heath on VE Day. We knew the top brass had arrived, but we didn't know what they were up to, but then the message came along. The war was over. Well it was one big party from then on. We had a huge bonfire and we danced round the CO singing 'For he's a jolly good fellow' until we were dizzy. He told us afterwards it was the most frightening moment of his life. He thought we were going to throw him on the fire.

Things started to wind down then. Those who had been in the war from the beginning were the first to be demobbed. I went to Spandau, where the war criminals were imprisoned. Then we were posted to Berlin, but we were ordered that we had to be spotless and smart when we went there. Everything had to be whitened. We worked on our belts and things until we were sick of it, then one of the men had this bright idea, soak everything in bleach. So we filled this tub with bleach and dropped all our webbing into it and everything disintegrated. It all came to bits in our hands.

The Germans were pleased to see us when we reached Berlin. We were the first British troops there and until then the Russians had been in charge. The Russian Women's Army guarded the streets and they carried machine guns.

Berlin was a mess. It had been bombed almost out of existence. There was so much rubble you couldn't get down some of the roads and you would see these German women patiently moving the rubble a bucket at a time. For the first four weeks we were there, the bomb damage was sprayed with disinfectant everyday.

Berlin was divided into zones. The Germans were not happy about the Russian zone. Some of them would shoot first and question after. There were often bodies lying in the gutter along the Unter den Linden. We had to do night duty at the police station because if they were called out to the Russian zone they would not go if they didn't have an army guard to protect them.

I was demobbed in June 1947. I missed the life and I missed the companionship, but I didn't really have time to think about it. I called in at the shop when I got home that first morning and the manager asked me if I could start back to work straight away, He was short staffed. It almost seemed there had never been a war and I had never been part of it, except that there were certain things that brought it all back. I couldn't stand the sound of a sewing machine. I had to go out if anyone used one because it sounded just like a moaning Minnie - the old mortars - you know.

Once Upon A Wartime III

Once Upon A Wartime III

John Stops a Tank.

On 27th August 1944, George was sitting down to lunch in his prisoner of war camp. It consisted of one thin slice of black bread, a bowl of watery soup in which floated tiny shreds of cabbage and two sad looking peas, a teaspoonful of milk powder and three mouthfuls of tinned pudding provided by the Red Cross. Early on in the war when he was captured and confined to Stalag VIIIb, the highlight of every week was the arrival of Red Cross parcels. These were distributed, one to each prisoner and joyfully opened. The contents were examined, discussed at length, exchanged where desirable and consumed over the next few days with grateful thanks by thousands of British and allied prisoners. Each parcel became a mini-banquet but without the glitter that accompanies such a feast. George claimed that ninety per cent of the men would probably have died of malnutrition had they not received Red Cross parcels.

By 1944, however, the situation was different. Communications all over Germany were chaotic. The road and railway systems had been relentlessly bombed and virtually wrecked, so it became almost impossible to move parcels to their destinations. The few that did find their way to the camps had to be shared, one parcel amongst eight or ten prisoners and then only once a month instead of weekly. The precious little food they received became precious indeed.

As George carefully spooned out his morsel of tinned pudding which was his share of one food parcel, he became aware of a strangely uncanny feeling, almost as though someone was trying to tell him something, but without putting it into words. He found it disturbing and worrying and immediately felt that John was involved.. Had anything happened to him? Was he in Normandy? BBC news bulletins were broadcast daily and prisoners of war listened to them in secret despite frequent attempts by the guards to discover how the news got through to them at all. So George knew that Normandy had been invaded by the allies some weeks ago and that the German army was in deep trouble and pulling back to re-group. Every POW was able to follow the progress of the British forces and their allies as they advanced through France.

Once Upon A Wartime III

Throughout his meagre lunch George, unable to shake off his concern resolved to remember the date, August 27th and carved it into a wooden plank of his bunk: 27 Aug 1944.

On 26th august, 'A' Company of the 7th Battalion, Somerset Light Infantry, commanded by a Major G and very under strength, had reached Vernon on the River Seine, northwest of Paris. I was 2nd in command. The Company had been ordered to cross the river and occupy a small house in a large forest which had been declared clear of enemy troops. We were given an approximate map reference and duly reached our objective, a deserted cottage. The Major immediately sent out a patrol and ordered the digging of slit trenches. My own job was to radio back to Battalion Headquarters. My signaller, Private Joe Guest, set up his portable radio in the kitchen and I sent a message reporting all was well.

It occurred to me that if perchance we were attacked, our men in the slit trenches would be completely hidden by bracken and therefore unable to fire their weapons at the enemy; for the same reason, the attackers would have nothing to fire at either, apart from the cottage. However, reconnaissance had combed the forest and declared it free of all enemy troops. I was able to indulge in my favourite hobby and spent a short while bird watching. George and I always took every opportunity to bird watch and that woodpecker I had heard might have been a new species to add to my list. Since joining the army we had seen many exotic species, most of them in India, a few in Palestine and Malta. George had seen one or two new European species from his POW camp in Germany.

The day passed quietly enough. Patrols went out at intervals, keeping to the many tracks and footpaths that meandered through the bracken, but with so few men in our force, only one patrol of men went out at a time. On the dot of every hour the signaller contacted Battalion Headquarters to report, solemnly, that there was nothing to report. When the trench digging was complete the men cleaned their weapons, checked their ammunition, or rested. I was thankful for this peaceful interlude after the fierce and noisome battles around Caen and Falaise, but the Major wisely drew up plans in the unlikely event of an attack.

Nightfall. Throughout the hours of darkness guards were posted and night patrols sent out. Those men not on duty slept fully dressed, on mattresses we had found in a cupboard. The Major and I shared the responsibility of waking Joe Guest every hour so he could report back to HQ. We also ensured that those on guard duty were fully alert. With over ten years of my army service behind me I was alert even when I was asleep. I believe I heard every owl that hooted that night. Twice I spoke to the sentries on guard and explained the different calls of different species of owl. They knew I was a bit dotty about birds.

Day dawned and we stood to, a customary practice at every dawn. On this occasion no warlike sound could be heard, no droning of planes, no booming of guns, no whine of shells passing over; only nature's own gentle sound of rustling leaves and twittering birds.

Then came breakfast, after which the Major inspected weapons, gave out a few orders and despatched a fresh patrol. The rest of the men settled down to what promised to be a repeat of the previous day; clear skies, warm sunshine, peace and quiet.

"One would think the war was over, " called out the Major as he joined me in the house.

"Maybe it is," I remarked happily. "I wouldn't mind staying here."

He stroked his chin, "Yes, I agree, it's a marvellous place, but shopping might be a problem."

"It might not be," I said, pulling a rather tattered and torn French map from its case which was covered in red chinagraph markings showing the distribution of our other companies. "Look, there's a village about a mile away, they're sure to have a greengrocer or a Marks and Spencers. You'd want a pub too, wouldn't you?"

"Wouldn't you?" the Major asked, laughing.

"No, not for me thanks," I replied, "I'm inclined to totter on a wine gum."

Our light hearted chatter continued for a while, until we discussed how best to keep the men occupied. They were sitting in groups cleaning their weapons, obviously enjoying their unaccustomed break from warfare.

The Major rose from his chair. "I have an idea," he said mysteriously as he went outside, without enlightening me.

I remained in the house with Joe Guest. He was a pleasant young man, well spoken, well mannered and better educated than most. He loved his job as a signaller and I had him in mind for promotion. He doubled as my batman. His cooking, though not quite up to cordon bleu standard, was distinctly superior to mine.

He disappeared into the kitchen. I spread my map over the table to check exactly where we were, but this proved impossible. Few tracks were shown whereas we had crossed many. The map was quite unreliable. Could we really be where we were supposed to be?

"Excuse me, Sir," called out Joe emerging from the kitchen and smiling happily. "Would you like baked beans or sausages for lunch, Sir?"

"Baked beans or sausages?" I repeated. "Why not baked beans and sausages?"

"Very good, Sir," he replied in a Jeeves like tone.

As it happens, we had neither. At that moment a shot rang out, then another and another. Joe and I instinctively flung ourselves to the floor. A machine gun opened fire and a string of bullets tore into the side of the house. Joe slithered into the kitchen for his radio, knowing I would want to send a message to HQ, but another volley from the machine gun shattered the window.

"Sir! Sir!" cried Joe, "I've been hit, I've been..." His voice faltering, trailed to a gasp. Joe was on the floor, blood spurting from a wound in his neck.

"Alright, Joe," I said as calmly as I could, "just lie quite still and let me deal with it."

Removing my first-aid dressing from its package, I applied it to the wound, but of course dared not bind it tightly. He started coughing and more blood spurted out and seeped through the dressing. I tied a second one over the first. In the meantime the firing continued and more bullets came whizzing into the room, ricocheting against the brick walls. Not wanting to lift him, I gently pushed and slid him into an alcove behind the stove which shielded him to some extent. Then I crept over to the wireless, thankful that I knew how to work it. Referring to my map, I made some quick calculations before calling up Battalion Headquarters.

"This is 'A' Company detachment calling, 'A' Company detachment calling... Captain Newmark speaking...we are under fire from all directions...machine gun firing from track in wood...map reference 450691...repeat, 450691...mortar fire requested at that map reference...also tank support along that track...track wide enough...also artillery fire on village one mile south of our position...suspect enemy occupation...reinforcements urgent...we have one casualty known, one casualty known...maybe others...stretcher bearers required...message ends."

"Wilco," came a voice at the other end. "Wilco, will comply."

It was good to know my message had got through and was understood. I crept back to Joe to reassure him. He lay quite still but was muttering softly.

"Joe, you're going to be alright; just keep still and don't talk now, wait till you are in hospital. I've asked for stretcher bearers so they should be here before long. Just keep still, you're doing very well." I hoped my voice was encouraging.

The firing had died down a bit and I crept over to the window. Slowly raising my head over the window sill, I saw to my amazement our men, including the Major, lined up in two rows, hands over their heads and being searched by German troops. Others were milling about nearby. It was clear we had been overrun.

I acted swiftly. I grabbed Joe's rifle, removed the bolt and stuffed it into a mattress. My revolver followed it. Then I removed all those coloured markings on my map and scribbled some false ones. Next I extracted some coded messages from my pocket and swallowed the lot. They were written on rice paper, not as tasty as baked beans and sausages, I reflected, but this was hardly the moment to start cooking. Finally, I went over to the wireless and stamped all over it, wondering whether anyone at HQ was listening in. I guessed someone outside the room would hear it and knew some German troops would be despatched to investigate.

I went over to Joe. "Stretcher bearers will be here soon," I told him, "and they will take care of you. You don't have to worry."

He smiled faintly. He was very pale, but didn't seem to be in pain. As far as I could tell the bleeding had stopped; that second dressing was clean. I placed a blanket over him, but didn't dare put one under his head to form a pillow. I didn't want to disturb his neck. I thought perhaps I should know his home address and fumbled for a piece of paper, but the door suddenly flung open and two German soldiers ordered me out at the point of two pistols.

"Raus! Raus!" shouted one of them, motioning to the door.

"I shall raus in a moment," I replied in a schoolmasterly voice. "Sprechen sie Deutsch? Voules-vous kindly attend to eine soldat in there. Kommen mit me."

I was determined to show them who was in charge and my sprinkling of German with a dash of French may have perplexed them. They had no distinguishing mark to indicate their rank, but to my great relief, I noticed one of them had a Red Cross haversack slung over his shoulder.

"Ah!" I said, pointing to it. "Kommen avec moi." I led the way into the kitchen. They both followed me and the medical orderly immediately knelt beside Joe, then spoke to his companion, urging him to call for stretcher-bearers. The second one then motioned me to the door. I was escorted out, knowing there was nothing more I could do. I joined the Major and the rest of our detachment, apart from those few who were on patrol somewhere. Hopefully, they would remain on patrol. I was quickly searched but nothing was taken from me, not even my binoculars which I had grabbed on my way out, together with a bar of chocolate which I held in one hand whilst my pockets were being examined.

By now German troops were all over the place prodding the bracken to make sure nobody was hiding. It was quite obvious we were outnumbered.

"How ever many are there?" I whispered to the Major as I stood beside him.

"Two to three hundred, I reckon. I don't know where they have come from, this whole area was declared free yesterday."

Very unfair, I thought. We had just 25 men. But there was no time to consider the fairness or unfairness of the situation for we were marched off in haste as a German Officer appeared. He was evidently in command for he shouted orders to his men and we found ourselves escorted by a formidable guard as we were marched along the track, that same track from which the machine gun had fired at us. Oh dear, I suddenly realised, I had asked for mortar fire to be directed along the track.

We and the first mortar shell arrived about the same time. "Stand still, British soldiers!" commanded a voice in perfect English.

We remained on the track, conscious of numerous rifles pointing at us to ensure we did not make a run for it. The German troops had flung themselves in ditches bordering the track and behind trees which provided flimsy protection from shells falling from above. Fortunately, most fell short of the target, some fell beyond it. Several Germans became casualties, yet we were unhurt, though one man had his water bottle pierced by shrapnel. The water gushed out and swamped his trousers. His language was unfit for publication when someone standing beside him suggested rudely that he couldn't wait.

Before long the shelling ended and stretcher bearers began moving about to search out the wounded. They were carried back along the track towards the house we had so recently occupied. I felt pleased. They would be collected from there, together with Joe Guest and taken to hospital.

In the meantime further orders were shouted. Our guards formed up alongside and we continued our march along that track. I was slightly nervous for I had asked for a tank to move up that track and sure enough, within minutes and as we were approaching a bend in the road, we could distinctly hear a rumble beyond the bend. I knew exactly what to expect.

"Stand still, British soldiers!" cried that same voice again as the Germans made themselves scarce, leaving us standing exposed to come what may. The rumble grew louder. The Major and I stood at the front of our column, so we were the first to see the gun barrel as the tank jerked round that bend, crunched forward a yard or two and suddenly stopped. The white star on its hulk, told us it was one of ours. We already had untold numbers of rifles aimed at us, now we had the muzzle of a gun pointing directly into our midst. If we lay down we risked being killed by the guards, if we remained standing, one shell would wipe out the lot of us.

I turned to the Major, "Have you read any good books lately?" I asked him in a loud voice, hoping somebody in the tank might hear me.

"Yes," he shouted back, "Tom Brown's School days."

Maybe that tank commander heard us. As we stood there we saw the turret slowly open, then inch by inch, a helmet appeared and a face, the mouth wide enough open to ungulate the tank. He obviously saw us, a group of soldiers bunched together on the track. Nobody else was in sight. I believed he guessed the truth, that we were prisoners being covered by our captors. He must have realised there was nothing much he could do, for he withdrew his head, the turret closed faster than it had opened and the tank reversed clumsily back round that bend and out of sight. We all remained still until the rumbling died away. We could breathe again and the German troops rose from their hiding places. They seemed as relieved as we were. We had all gone through a nerve wracking experience and the Germans, having shared it with us, were slightly more cordial towards us. I had the impression they admired our calm behaviour.

There was a further bout of shouting of orders and guards surrounding us. This time we were marched back in the other direction, back towards the house. The German commander had evidently had enough of that wood. Everyone moved back at a fairly brisk pace and on reaching the house I was greatly relieved to see a number of ambulances there and medical orderlies attending the wounded. It was my turn to admire the efficiency of their troops. I wanted to ask about Joe Guest, but we were marched straight past the house, out of the wood and into the open country and we didn't stop moving until we reached the village I had asked to be shelled by our artillery! Fortunately the shelling had already taken place. We were shepherded into a large barn which had escaped any damage and there we spent the rest of the day and that night. The guards fed us reasonably well and indeed shared their rations with us. Some spoke broken English and admitted they could not win the war. They told us they were retreating from the front and trying desperately to make their way back to Deutschland. They were, in fact, lost and only came upon us by accident! They took us captive largely to raise their morale. They fully expected to become prisoners themselves before long, so it was in their own interest to treat us well. I think perhaps we felt a bit sorry for them even though we were their prisoners.

During the next six days we were escorted across miles of northeast France, fed not only by the German army but also by the French people who showered us with delicious French loaves, masses of fruit and other sustenance including wine! Even so, it was not all plain sailing. Each day we were joined by more prisoners, mainly French soldiers. Our numbers grew to several hundred and, as we travelled across the country in a long column we made a conspicuous target from the air and that was where the danger lay. Our own aircraft, Spitfires and Hurricanes, were roaming the skies, shooting at anything that looked like Germans retreating. The pilots couldn't tell whether we were friendly or hostile. To avoid being mown down by any aircraft, two German sentries moved ahead of the column and two well to the rear. If they sighted a plane even on the horizon, they would blow their whistles and the entire column, prisoners and guards alike would fall flat on the ground, face down and lie motionless. It happened several times and on each occasion we all studied the ground at close quarters and hoped we blended into it. The strategy was effective for not one of the many planes that flew over us returned to have another look. By deliberately appearing lifeless, we avoided becoming lifeless.

After six perilous days trudging across the corner of France we reached a town which lay in ruins. It was Amiens and here our walk ended at what was once a railways station but was now a shambles. Even so, a train was waiting, not a passenger train nor a freight train, but a cattle train with dozens of box cars or cattle trucks assembled there to transport us into Germany. By crafty manoeuvring the Major managed to keep us altogether and we were herded into one box car, no mean feat, bearing in mind there were now about 600 prisoners milling about the remains of a platform or fighting their way into the cleanest looking cattle trucks. I had hoped our fairly amiable guards would accompany us, but my hopes were soon dashed.

It was dark before the train pulled noisily out of the station. I was amazed the lines were in good enough condition for any train to go anywhere but no doubt some had been repaired, if only temporarily for we jogged and jolted along painfully slowly through the night, stopping at every station and between stations. Swarms of country folk bombarded us with bread, cheese and other delights, regardless of the hour. Do the French ever go to sleep, I wondered. We reasoned why the guards allowed their generosity. As long as the French supplied us with food, they wouldn't have to. One gentleman handed me a packet of cigarettes. "Merci beaucoup," I said, "je no smokay pas mais he will donnerai to my friends. Also, voules-vous post this lettre si'l vous plait and merci encore, je suis trés grateful." I handed him a letter to my parents and months later I learned that it had reached them safely. To this day I remain trés grateful.

Our train journey lasted four days and nights. At intervals the prisoners were permitted to leave their wagons in order to spend pennies by the wayside and under heavy guard. Otherwise we were confined to the crowded conditions inside the four walls of our truck. The small barred and broken windows provided some ventilation, but we found a further use for them. .Whenever British or American planes swooped low over the train to examine us, as they frequently did, we held out a variety of white materials to indicate that we were prisoners of war, not a train load of German troops. Handkerchiefs, vests, pants, even bandages fluttered in the breeze warning the pilots to hold their fire, we were not a target. Who would have thought a few hundred pairs of pants and vests played a crucial role in World War II crucial to us, anyway.

It was a different story at night when we were shunted into sidings. Railways sidings were main targets for heavy bombers and on two successive nights we experienced the horrors of a bombing raid. We were left locked inside our wagons whilst our guards sheltered wherever they could. Explosions rocked the train frequently and we hoped bomb blasts might at least damage the walls of the truck and give us a chance to escape. It was pure chance we were not blown sky high. Thousands of trains were destroyed in night raids over France and Germany, but some guardian angels must have hovered over ours during those two nights. The whole train was left intact though there were huge bomb craters up and down the line, tracks torn asunder, signals out of action, wreckage everywhere. How any trains moved at all was a mystery, but hordes of workmen were able to patch up the tracks to enable a few trains to struggle through to their destinations. Ours was one of those few. I like to think my white pants waving merrily from the window by day helped to save us.

It was late on the fifth morning that our train finally reached its destination. A battered nameplate indicated we had arrived at Limburg. We were ordered out by our guards, handed over to a new set of German Officers and men who escorted us to a prisoner of war camp not far away. This proved to be a holding camp where all the prisoners were sorted out according to nationalities, commissioned ranks and other ranks, so here the Major and I had to part company with our men. They would go on to a Stalag, we two to an Oflag. The men were in good spirits, however, who wouldn't be after being confined to a wagon for four days and nights! After sharing so many hardships and hazards with them it was a pity we could not spend the rest of the war together. But we were survivors and looked forward to the many reunions that were bound to take place once the war was over. My one lasting regret was that Joe Guest, my faithful signaller, was absent, but I knew he would be receiving better treatment in hospital than we would in a prisoner of war camp.

After a short and comparatively uneventful journey the Major and I entered the gates of Oflag 79 near Brunswick, our 'home' for the rest of the war. We were lucky, our POW camp had once been some Luftwaffe barracks and therefore fairly substantial buildings with two floors. With winter approaching this was important. We soon made friends amongst the 2000 or so officers already 'in the bag' and from them we learnt what to expect. The Germans were losing the war and they knew it. For this reason the guards tended to treat us with a degree of lenience rather than harshness. Many were elderly grey haired veterans and astute enough to comply with the rules of the Geneva Convention. They were well aware that it would not be so very long before they would be changing places with us. The German Officers must have known that we were listening to the BBC daily news broadcasts every day without fail. They must have known we were bribing the guards for extra food and small luxuries and, that we were placing hundreds of home made candles in every window at night time whenever our planes flew over on bombing missions. The candles, made from tins of butter and a short length of pyjama cord, served to warn the pilots that we, not the Luftwaffe, were occupying their barracks.

In a strange sort of way, I personally felt almost happy to be experiencing similar conditions to those that George had suffered for nearly five years. I did in fact write a letter to Hitler asking for George to be transferred to my camp, but never had a reply. However, for both of us to be prisoners of war simply meant that we were becoming more 'twinnish' than ever and would have that much more to talk about once we were back home.

Once Upon A Wartime III

At the end of the war, George and I were released from our respective camps on the same day and arrived home within an hour of each other. Family celebrations lasted the rest of that day, but at length we were able to talk quietly together and to discuss some of the events of those five years of separation.

George suddenly remembered a question he had had on his mind for some months. "Do you remember the date you were captured?" he asked.

Slightly surprised at this apparently trivial question, I had to think back to that fateful day, when Joe Guest had enquired about my choice for lunch, baked beans or sausages. It was late summer.

"Yes, near the end of August," I replied. "Why do you want to know?"

"What was the exact date?" George persisted, ignoring my question. I knew from his tone that he had something to divulge.

I thought back again. We had reached Vernon, crossed the river and were in the forest. That was August 26th. "It would have been the 27th August," I said firmly.

"I knew it! I knew it all along!" He exclaimed excitedly. "I even carved the date into my bunk. I was having lunch when I had a strange feeling, a sort of presentiment that something had happened to you. It even spoilt my lunch. But I wonder how I knew."

"My lunch was spoilt too," I said wistfully. "How on earth could you have known? I wonder if it had something to do with being identical twins. I wonder."

We both wondered.

(Joe Guest survived his wounds and was released from hospital when Brussels was over run. He died some 40 years later.)

Once Upon A Wartime III

Above: *A postcard sent from George om 11th December 1941 from Stalag VIII B Gepruit*

Below: *George, left, John, right, after their release from POW camps*

George Stops a Bullet

By the time World War II started in September 1939, we had already been in the army for six years serving with the Queen's Own Royal West Kent Regiment at Aldershot and Shorncliffe, then overseas with the 1st Battalion in India, Palestine and Malta. We were stationed in Malta at the outbreak of war and, very soon afterwards we were both promoted to unpaid Lance-Sergeant, Acting Sergeant and War Substantive Sergeant all in one day. The army moves in mysterious ways.

A few weeks later, the army moved again, far more drastically as far as we were concerned. We were separated. Until now we had always managed to stay together in the Regiment, despite the efforts of a few noncommissioned officers to separate us. Now Hitler had succeeded where others had failed, even though he never knew it. The authorities decreed that Sergeant George Newmark be posted to the United Kingdom where he would be required to train the many new recruits joining up for the duration. Sergeant John Newark remained in Malta until 1941, when he too returned to the UK to take a commission, but by then George was a prisoner or war in Germany, which he describes in letters home.

Dear Edward

This is the first official letter I've been allowed to write and, although I've written two brief letters I doubt if they will ever reach you, so I shall begin again from May 20th.

First of all, before I start, you may like to know that I am perfectly safe, very much alive and thrilled to death.

Now on May 20th, my battalion went to a town called (the name had been blackened out by the German censors) in north France. Minutes after our arrival we all collected in the main square and awaited orders and, minutes later, along comes the German army! They came in hundreds of tanks and the first thing we saw was a tank peering round each road leading into the square. Next moment there was a battle royal. We all fled behind cover, some into buildings, some behind lorries. Everyone opened fire on the Germans and they fired at us with machine guns, shells and everything else.

I was behind one of our lorries, another vehicle opposite was in flames and, for a moment I couldn't see a thing through all the smoke. Then one of our men nearby was wounded in the arm. He came over to me and just as I was about to bandage him up, something like a flat iron hit me in the chest. My right arm was completely numb and although I knew I had been wounded, I somehow felt perfectly normal, no pain whatsoever. Later, I ran from behind my lorry into a large school and, there I removed my equipment and tunic, just to see if I had been wounded, as I still felt perfectly normal, except for the numbness in my arm. To my surprise I found that a bullet had gone right through my chest; luckily it had missed my lung, also my ribs, but it had not come out the other side. I put on a first field dressing and decided to await the arrival of Aunt Mabel (a family aunt).

Before long the building in which I had taken cover began to get shelled, so with six other men I retired to the cellar. There we remained for an hour or so until the firing ceased. A few minutes later we heard footsteps outside the cellar and a lot of talking. The talking was German! I died instantly. We were out of sight of course in our cellar, although there was only a short flight of steps leading down to us. Nevertheless, we decided to remain where we were and as soon as the Germans left the building we would do likewise and hide somewhere until nightfall.

Unfortunately, the Germans did not leave the building. They made it their headquarters! So we remained in our cellar all that day, all that night and all the following day. The next night we decided to take off our boots, creep upstairs and jump out of a window into the street. This we did successfully and found ourselves in a street littered with burnt out lorries and other wreckage.

It was bright moonlight so we hurried along the road in our socks, hiding in the shadows every time we saw any German troops. At last we reached the open country, so we put on our boots and just went! I tried to find the Pole Star but couldn't, so we continued to walk, hoping we were going in a southerly direction. We walked across country all night, breaking into a house at one point. Here we found bread, sugar and cocoa and, more important to me, a large roll of cotton wool and several crepe bandages.

One of the men put a dressing on my wound which was now becoming rather painful. It was roughly one inch across and several inches into me, but I knew no serious injury had been done as I felt otherwise in the best of health.

Next morning at dawn we broke into another house and decided to sleep there all day and to travel only at night. So after making some cocoa we went to bed, seven of us in four beds. I had a spring bed, sheets, blankets and eiderdown complete and into it I climbed, fully dressed, boots and everything.

Once Upon A Wartime III

That evening about six o'clock along came the German army in hundreds of lorries, travelling along the road outside. The six men all peeped out of the windows, but I just stayed in bed and quaked, and I quaked more when one of the lorries stopped right outside our house. We quickly locked the door, pushed a bed up against it and hid in the cupboards, in the beds and under them. A few Germans walked into the house. We heard them open the drawers in the next room. Then one of them turned the handle and found it locked. They went outside. A moment later we heard the shutters of our windows being opened. I ceased to exist, our discovery was imminent. The windows were thrown open and peering through the sheets under which I was hiding, I saw the outline of a German about to climb in. He got half way, then suddenly jumped out again and ran off. He had evidently seen us. We emerged from our beds and cupboards and awaited the arrival of whomever he had gone to fetch.

About eight German troops climbed in through the window.

"How do you," I said.

One of them spoke English and asked who we were, whether we were armed and various other questions. He then asked if we were hungry and promptly gave us chocolate, cigarettes, cigars, wine, beer, biscuits and bread and told us to make ourselves at home! I told him about my wound and he went off to find a doctor.

To cut a long story short, the six men were taken to a place some twenty miles north and I was taken to hospital. There I received good treatment and for the first time in ten days my case was considered to be quite serious as the bullet was evidently still in me, there being only one hole. The wound began to heal however and they decided the bullet must have come out during my few days at large. The food was extremely tasty but only two meals a day, at one o'clock and seven o'clock. I thinned considerably and demanded Ovaltine which of course I never received. After three weeks in the hospital my wound reached the sticking plaster stage and that takes me up to yesterday, June 12th.

Well, yesterday I was told to collect all my belongings which consisted of only a mess tin, a shaving kit which I had found and one blanket. Outside were some thirty open lorries and into them several hundred patients, all walking cases, clambered. We had no idea of our destination. We started off in a north-easterly direction, passing literally hundreds of wrecked cars, buses, tanks and other vehicles lying in the ditches and on the roadside practically on top of one another.

Later on we crossed into Belgium and passed through several large towns including Charleroi and Liege. These places, unlike the French towns which were deserted, were more or less normal. Shops were open, people thronged the streets and threw cigarettes and chocolate into our lorries, everyone seemed quite happy. On we went across rivers, through hilly country, delightful scenery all the way. Then we entered another town, but this time every house had a swastika flag flying and the shops had German names. We were in Germany. Everybody was very curious to see us, some showed sympathy, some horror, but most people just showed ordinary curiosity.

However, passing through the town twice, the drivers made some enquiries and finally arrived back in Belgium at a place I am not allowed to name. We were put into a large disused factory and our beds are of straw. We still get medical treatment of some sort but I do my own now. The meals consist mostly of small aniseed biscuits and hot weak coffee without milk. Whilst in hospital we had two very well cooked meals a day, usually beef or mutton with potatoes or tapioca or macaroni, very nice but not nearly enough. I was permanently hungry and of course there were no shops or anything. Here we get hundreds of these little aniseed biscuits, so although we are never hungry, the quality is not as good as it was in hospital.

Well now I must close. Soon I'll be in a permanent prison camp in Germany and I expect to be able to write regularly and you will be able to write back. I believe I shall be allowed to write once a month. When I am settled down you must let me know all the recent news of the war as we don't know a thing. Also please send a one ton slab of chocolate.

Goodbye for now and don't expect another letter until it comes. We may move anywhere, I hope it will be a nice spot - the Bavarian Alps! And remember in war time no news is good news. When I return to England, I shall require a massive steak and kidney pudding.
Love George

That bullet eventually came to light some weeks later when George could feel a small hard lump in his back, roughly in the centre. In due course it was examined by a doctor.

"Ja, ja," exclaimed the doctor, as he pressed and probed with a finger. "I can feel eins, zwei bullets, not one bullet, two bullets you have in your back. I vill consult my colleague. You vill vait till tomorrow and if my colleague come, he will remove ze bullets. Don't worry, they vill not hurt so much coming out as they did going in." He laughed loudly at his little joke.

"Danke schon," said George in passable German. He was not a bit worried about the pain, but was totally mystified about there being two bullets. He felt there must be some mistake.

The mystery was solved the next day when a gentleman wearing a white coat gave George a local anaesthetic and a few minutes later deftly removed first half a bullet, then the other half.

"Here is ze bullet!" he cried in triumph, "but it is broken in two pieces."

"Ah, now I understand why the other doctor thought there were two bullets," George explained. "Thank you very much Herr Doctor and dancke very schon. I would like to keep the bullet if you don't mind," he added, helping himself to both halves. "After all, it was, in a sense, a present. Thank you again, Herr Doctor."

"Ja, ja, you can have ze bullet. By the way, I am not a doctor. I am a - how you say - I am a vet!"

Extracts from some of George's other letters written from his prison camp now follow. Most of them were addressed to his Mother, but not always with her correct initials. When George was moved from one prison camp to another as happened occasionally, Mother found herself addressed with a variety of initials on successive letters, thus, Mrs F R Newmark, Mrs E U newmark, Mrs D E N Newmark, Mrs T Newmark, Mrs A L Newmark. Mother of course realised George was telling her something and guessed it was informing her of his whereabouts. She was right, the initials in this case spelt out the location of his new prison camp, Freudenatal.

These particular letters together with that shattered bullet and a small notebook through which the bullet went and George's war medals, are now on display in the Redoubt Museum, Eastbourne.

It is worth recording that John Newmark had stayed in Malta and had no way of knowing that his brother was sending secret messages home. Yet when he too was captured after the Normandy landing and finished up in a prison camp in Germany, he devised exactly the same method of letting his parents know his location. Identical twins do evidently think alike.

Extracts from George's letters home

July 3rd 1940. I am now in a British prisoners camp in Germany. The German guards treat us very well, they are nothing like you see in films! My address is: Sergeant G Newmark, 15903, Stalag VIIIb, Deutschland. My wound is now completely healed and I am perfectly well but rather thin! Please write giving me our new home address and any news of John. Your letters will be strictly censored so be careful what you say about the war, but let me know that everyone thinks it will soon be over. Tell John everything and my address. Wish you could send me a Lyons cream cake. Hope war ends before winter.

August 23rd 1940. I am still keeping well enough, though the weather has become distinctly wintry already, our rooms however are fairly warm. When it begins to get too cold I shall simply retire to my bed and only emerge for meals. Still no sign of any ladies or parcels yet, pity I'm not on the telephone! My socks have now reached the stage when I can put them on from either end.

September 5th 1940. There were no letter cards issued last week so I was unable to write. We have been informed that the mail between Germany and England is now normal. Several men have received letters dated around July and more are expected daily, so I hope to have some any day now. Also a few parcels from the Red Cross arrived in the camp this week though they didn't go far between 1000 men. I had a taste of meat stew flavoured Marmite and a cup of tea. There was also a twopenny bar of Cadbury's chocolate between 56 men, so we drew for it and, of course I lost. I saw it however, which was something! Apart from that my news is as little as usual. We continue to be treated very well and the other day we all had an inoculation the same as we would have had in our own army. It hurt less too!

November 28th 1941. (A new site) I have been here a week during which I have done more work than in the rest of my life. We are 60 miles from Stalag VlllB in mountainous country which I believe Gerda would know (Gerda, an Austrian lady, is a sister-in-law). The work consists of putting haystacks into a machine which turns it out again all square and tied up in bundles. Our billets are extremely good. We live in a little village up in the clouds and our room is fitted with a stove and an oven.

February 8th 1942. I'm suffering another cakeless birthday, still I think it will be the last.

May 31st 1942. John when you next write will you let me know exactly when I'm coming home, because if it is not soon I shall demand a visitors day. This week we all received Red Cross parcel, the first since February. I managed to make myself a brunch, complete except for the egg. Exquisite.

June 21st 1942. Edward's letter said that John had been accepted for an Officer Cadet Training Unit. I shall therefore prepare myself to remain a prisoner for 30 years!

June 28th 1942. One letter from John this week dated May 23rd. Last week I became a lumberjack for a day. Six of us had to go to a forest about three miles away where some men were felling trees. Our job was to collect the branches and pile them just off the roadway. I watched about 20 pine trees cut down, dragged a few of the smallest branches off the road and then went off looking for beetles. We spent the whole day in the forest and I thoroughly enjoyed it except for the gnats which nearly ate me.

Once Upon A Wartime III

September 6th 1942. Last week, for the first time since I arrived in Germany, I heard a warbling sound (air-raid siren). Having no steel helmet, I prepared to don the wash basin, but nothing happened so I returned to slumber. I'm expecting your May parcel any week now, they're very slow.

November 8th 1942. Once again no mail this week. We've heard all about the doings of the 8th Army which has cheered me up considerably, so much in fact that the last room I painted, a bathroom, I did in vivid orange, (George had volunteered to work as a house painter. When asked by the German authorities what experience he had had, he claimed to have painted the railings outside Buckingham Palace. The authorities were duly impressed and he was given the job).

November 1942. Tomorrow I am returning to the Stalag for a short period in hospital, my ailment being yellow jaundice. Actually, I have had it for ten days and am nearly better, but the doctors here said I must go into the Stalag hospital for a while in order to receive the correct diet. I asked if I could go to hospital here, but the doctor said nein as I was not urgent. I said I was urgent, so he said I was not an accident. I agreed I wasn't an accident.

November 27th 1942. I am now in the main Stalag and just about to go into hospital. I have everything except a bunch of grapes.

December 5th 1942. I have now been in the Stalag hospital just a week and my yellow jaundice is fast departing. Congratulations to Mabel and Bill on their silver anniversary. I hope I'm home for the golden.

December 7th 1942. Here I am, about to spend my third Christmas. I'm still in hospital trying to get rid of the last traces of yellow jaundice. I have had the illness exactly four weeks, I actually felt ill the first week, but didn't go yellow and by the 12th day when I went into hospital, I was brilliant. I shone for about six days, then it started to fade and now there's just a tiny bit in my eyes. I've had no pain, not even a headache, in fact I've quite enjoyed it. Well, Christmas is upon us and still no turkey. Two or three of your recent letters have hinted at the possibility of the war ending, so I am now packed. On arrival home I hope to be confronted with yard-long sausages and mash. Aching to know if John is an officer yet.

January 17th 1943. I have almost reached the ripe old age of 30. I must develop wrinkles. Last week we moved to our new billets which are very comfortable and roomy. We built the hut ourselves and had to put up the barbed wire

Once Upon A Wartime III

enclosure. When an officer inspected the place he found numerous gaps in the wire, so German troops had to re-wire it.

March 14th 1943. I was surprised to hear that John had pneumonia recently, I had fondly imagined that, being an officer he would have been advancing, sword out thrust. Today we planted our first seeds, onions and parsnips in the vegetable garden, pansies and dahlias in the flower beds. Charming.

April 11th 1943. Last week a mystery befell me, I received a parcel of 500 cigarettes! The enclosed card mentioned the sender as St Germaine's School, which deepens the mystery.

April 18th 1943. Another 500 cigarettes from my unknown admirer! We bought over 100 plants including lupins, delphiniums, roses, forget-me-nots and many others I can't spell. We've also sown thousands of seeds, both flower and vegetable.

May 9th 1943. This week I had cause to protest. Until recently my job, as you know, has been painting, though there has been little to do these last few weeks. So now my boss has said that I could do another job. I asked him what it was and he said it would be coal-heaving. I told him not to be so foolish. Besides, I said, nobody who came from Hampstead ever heaved coal. I was told, however, that I would be on coal-heaving and would I kindly fall in with the others at once, ready to march down to the station. I said I would be delighted and selecting the tiniest shovel available, I fell in. We marched to the station and there I beheld the coal which had to be heaved - a train load! I just sank to the ground, aghast and promptly wished myself stricken with mumps. Just as I was calculating how many years the job would last, I saw the train begin to move, leaving one wagon of coal behind. The guard told us to start. Coal heaving is certainly hard work, even though I heaved only one lump at a time. I am glad to hear that Mrs T Uniss is free from her attack of German measles.

June 6th 1943. I'm back on my painting job again. Last week I did a doctor's bedroom and bathroom and now I'm on the hospital where he is in charge. There are about ten rooms, corridors and more bathrooms. I shall do the mortuary orange with a pattern of purple bunches of grapes.

September 12th 1943. Everybody here is delighted with the news though we only hear a few bare facts. One man has already packed his kit ready to go home. Our garden is still utterly charming though many of the flowers are dying off. You mentioned weeding is your strong point. I also do a lot, but instead of pulling the weeds out, I find it much quicker to push them in about a yard with a broom handle! I'm hoping the war will end before they come up again.

October 24th 1943. One day last week we all had to go to the station to unload a wagon of coal. It so happened that the wagon next to it was an open one, so I peeped over the top and beheld apples. Quite absent-mindedly, I took one, nobody said I mustn't and I found it very much to my liking. So I took another, followed by a third. To cut a long story short, everyone else took sufficient to last till next April or thereabouts. In addition, stewed apple is on the menu three times a week.

November 7th 1943. During the week we heard a faint rumour concerning the possible exchange of prisoners. As soon as I heard it I packed. I shall be extremely indignant if I am swopped for anybody else below a general. The Geneva Convention says something about men who have been prisoners a long time may be exchanged or sent to a neutral country, but it does not say what constitutes a long time. Most people agree that three years is a long time, some say five years. Personally, I consider two weeks to be an age, whilst three years is not so much a long time as a life time. I heard from Big Ben yesterday who told me that Mrs Keeve had recovered from a nasty disease.

November 14th 1943. I am now preparing to spend my fourth turkeyless Christmas here, though it may not be quite turkeyless, I have my eye on a bird owned by a farm not far away.

November 23rd 1943. We have been amusing ourselves recently by playing chess, a game at which I shine. We organised a chess tournament and you will be pleased to hear I won it. There was no prize so I took the day off. But when we had a 100 yard race during the summer I came in last and took three days off.

January 9th 1944. I've just received your letter of November 25th telling me of Harry Sallar's visit, (A friend of George sent home from the prison camp). I'm glad you have now had a first hand account of prison life, though as yet you probably know very little about life on a working party. Vastly amusing, I can assure you. No doubt you satisfied yourself that my wound is only a memory and a scar, though when I received it I thought a piano had gone through me! Did Harry tell you of my efforts to pass the medical officer who told me what to say when I went before the board? And how, when the board sat, this same medical officer was in charge of it and said I hadn't a hope of passing? Still, it is better to be here fit than in England, permanently unfit. I still can't decide what to do after the war, in fact I've decided not to decide what to do after the war until after the war.

February 8th 1944. Dear John, Many merry returns of the day. So far I have received a pair of shoes and a pair of socks, very very nice too. Second hand of course, but nevertheless, very very nice too. I also made the guard wish me many happy returns before I got up. MacDougall is making me a cake with 31 matches on it.

February 13th 1944. This morning I had fried bread and eggs for breakfast, but the eggs, alas, were purely imaginary.

February 27th 1944. One of the men here causes considerable merriment not only because he sometimes wears his old school tie, an extremely faded and tattered article, but who is forever proclaiming the fact that caviare should be provided for all prisoners. Furthermore his name is Cobblestone!

April 2nd 1944. I have planned to go shopping at Selfridges on August 7th, after lunch. For the last three years I have daily planned and imagined my arrival home, recently, however, I have done my planning and imagining not daily but hourly. I have even planned such details as which side of the taxi to sit on. I've decided the left side for no reason at all other than the delight of planning it.

June 4th 1944. I am Head gardener now and I intend the garden to be one of the sights, that is if the war lasts long enough. At the moment it looks as though it will continue another two or three years. If it is still on by 1960, I shall contemplate escaping. I shall just walk out of the gate, turn left and continue walking.

In the chaos and confusion after the second front opened up with the invasion of Normandy and the subsequent bombing of roads and railways and other lines of communications, very few letters were received from George, nor indeed by him.
Interestingly enough, John also spent time in his prison camp planning and imagining his arrival home at the end of the war. Most prisoners would have had similar thoughts, but both George and John went into some details and, being identical twins, most of the details were identical including John's decision to sit on the left had side of the taxi home, a decision taken without any foundation other than the joy of planning it.